The Birdcatcher

Also by Gayl Jones

FICTION

Corregidora (novel) (1975)
Eva's Man (novel) (1976)
White Rat (short stories) (1977)
The Healing (novel) (1998)
Mosquito (novel) (1999)
Palmares (novel) (2021)

POETRY COLLECTIONS

The Hermit-Woman (1983)
Xarque and Other Poems (1985)
Song for Anninho (1999)
Song for Almeyda and Song for Anninho (2022)

OTHER WORKS

Chile Woman (play) (1974)
Liberating Voices: Oral Tradition in African American Literature
  (criticism) (1991)

The Birdcatcher

GAYL JONES

BEACON PRESS

Boston

BEACON PRESS
Boston, Massachusetts
www.beacon.org

Beacon Press books
are published under the auspices of
the Unitarian Universalist Association of Congregations.

25 24 23 22   8 7 6 5 4 3 2 1

This book is printed on acid-free paper that meets the uncoated
paper ANSI/NISO specifications for permanence as revised in 1992.

Text design by Michael Starkman at
Wilsted & Taylor Publishing Services

First published as *Die Vogelfangerin by Rowohlt*
(Neue Frau imprint), Hamburg, Germany: January 1986
(translated into German from the English language manuscript).

Names: Jones, Gayl, author.
Title: The birdcatcher / Gayl Jones.
Description: Boston : Beacon Press, [2022] | Summary: "Set primarily on the
    island of Ibiza, the story is narrated by the writer Amanda Wordlaw,
    whose closest friend, a gifted sculptor named Catherine Shuger, is
    repeatedly institutionalized for trying to kill a husband who never
    leaves her. The three form a quirky triangle on the white-washed
    island"— Provided by publisher.
Identifiers: LCCN 2022010991 | ISBN 9780807029947 (hardcover ; acid-free
    paper) | ISBN 9780807030004 (ebook)
Subjects: LCGFT: Novels.
Classification: LCC PS3560.O483 B57 2022 |
    DDC 813/.54—dc23/eng/20220318
LC record available at https://lccn.loc.gov/2022010991

For my editors,
Angela Praesent (1945–2009)
and Helene Atwan

If I'm set on getting islands,
Others are set on worse.

—SANCHO PANZA

Book I   *How to Catch Foxes*

1

Ibiza. I have left Brazil and am living on the white-washed island of Ibiza with my friend Catherine Shuger, a sculptor who has been declared legally insane, and her husband, Ernest, a freelance writer of popular science articles. We are all expatriate Americans: exiles.

Standing on the terrace, sheltered in the smell of oranges and eucalyptus, washed in sunlight, you'd swear this was a paradise. But to tell the truth the place is full of dangers. The dangers, however, are not directed toward me but toward Ernest. You see, Catherine sometimes tries to kill her husband. It has been this way for years: He puts her into an asylum, thinks she's well, takes her out again, and she tries to kill him. He puts her in another one, thinks she's well, takes her out again, she tries to kill him: on and on. You'd think we'd learn by now; you'd think everybody'd learn, don't you? But somehow we keep the optimism, or the pretense, bring her out, and wait. She's like the fucking trapdoor spider.

Here she's sitting now: We're both out on the dandelion-bright terrace. I'm writing this, and Catherine's scribbling in her therapy notebook that her last psychiatrist told her to keep. Ernest is inside behind the glass door working on an article on laser medicine. Here Catherine sits in a pink silk nightie and blue flannel housecoat, though it's two o'clock in the afternoon and hot as fresh cow dung out here. Underneath I know what she's wearing too—Lady Jockey drawers (Look, Amanda, Jockey makes drawers for women! I've got to get some of these!) and a champagne-colored (champagne!) Danskin bra. And looking so sweet! If you didn't know her story, well, you could eat her up the way she's looking now: wrist on her chin, her jaws as innocent and plum as cherubs'.

Astronomers say that even galaxies eat each other; so why not let's eat this sweet bitch?

Anyway, she tries to kill Ernest: that's all the story really. No one knows why, and Catherine won't tell. The rest of us can only list the attempts: Once she tried to dump a steel bookcase on him, another time she lunged at him with a red-hot poker; once she grabbed the rusty spoke of a bicycle wheel when we were passing by a salvage dump in Detroit.

We were walking down this deserted backstreet one Sunday, before noon. When Catherine spotted the salvage dump, she ran a bit ahead of us, to the wire-mesh fence. When we got to her, she had her hands entwined in the fence. We stood behind her, watching. She looked almost like a little girl in her yellow cotton dress, her hair in tiny braids and tied with a ribbon, her bowlegs peeking out of the dress and looking as if she were perpetually getting ready to climb onto a saddle—with ride-'em-cowgirl bowlegs. She was even wearing socks with her high-heeled shoes—that was the latest style. Standing pigeon-toed, she looked like a canary peeking into its cage.

"Come along, Catherine," Ernest said, after we had stood there a moment.

"I'm looking to see if they've got anything I can use. They've got a lot of rubber things. I'm thinking of maybe doing a series of pieces in rubber. Bouncing the idea around, you know."

She seemed in delightful good humor for a change.

I stopped watching her and watched the pale building that was the central office for the salvage company. It had high windows, so you'd have to climb a ladder to peek inside. The door was tall and narrow; only one person could enter at a time. I imagined one of those slender carnival giants—a man who lived on stilts—the sort you see in carnival parades, wearing a tuxedo and an oversized stove-pipe hat.

"We'll come back tomorrow and you can look around."

I turned; Catherine turned, one foot darted forward, she stretched her arm like a fencer, looking as determined as an expert. But Ernest had done something she hadn't counted on; he had already taken off his leather jacket and had draped it over his arm—luck or premonition I don't know—so that he had a ready-made shield against her. She stabbed the leather. I grabbed her from behind around the waist and held. She still stood with one leg jutted forward; the other foot had fallen out of its shoe, so she was off-balance, easy for me to hold. Ernest got the bicycle spoke out of her hand and just stood looking. She gave a sudden yell like a samurai, then settled into my arms. A weird, curious look on Ernest. Like that time I went with an aunt to the police department to file a complaint. There was another woman there sitting at a gray, metal table, examining photographs. She kept turning pages till she got to the page where she saw the familiar face. "This is him," she said, then, "I think this is him. This could quite possibly be him." The detective standing behind her said, "We don't go by possibly in here." When my aunt and I got outside, she said, "That's not exactly true that they don't go by possibly. I have known them to go by possibly." Anyway, the look of that woman spotting the "possibly" photograph was the look that Ernest had watching Catherine: "This is her. I think this is her. This could quite possibly be her." But, standing behind Catherine's shoulder, it was as if he were looking at both her and me at the same time.

Finally, he took the bicycle spoke and tossed it over the fence. It dangled on top of a pile of junk, like an antenna.

"I know where they mend leather," Catherine said.

I let go of her.

Ernest folded his jacket, so the hole in it wasn't visible. "So where do you folks want to go for lunch?" he asked.

"I want Greektown," said Catherine.

"I'd like to hear where Amanda wants to go. You like Chinese, don't you?" he asked.

"Greektown's fine," I said.

"Greektown then," he said, scratching the side of his neck and blowing air out of his mouth, sounding like a tire deflating.

So every time she tries something now it's new, like an inspiration. In the beginning it used to always be knives, then we stopped allowing knives, not real ones, not even rubber ones. Now she has to improvise.

And Ernest has to carry her doctor's reports everywhere they go, so he doesn't have to keep explaining. He carries around xeroxed copies in brown manila envelopes. In fact, I've got a couple of her doctor's reports in my suitcase.

If Catherine is the trapdoor spider, Ernest is . . . How can I describe him? He's lovely. Cinnamon-colored with big shoulders. I call him "big two-hearted river." You have to have two hearts to take care of a difficult woman like Catherine. And my husband thought I was a witch! I'm a unicorn compared to her.

When Catherine isn't looking sweet she's looking like she's standing behind glass. I guess that's because she's spent so many fucking days standing behind glass. What would you expect? They won't even let her take her compact when she goes to those places, you see because it's got a mirror in it, and they're afraid she might break the mirror, harm herself, cut her wrists or something. But it's not herself she tries to harm, never herself. They could let her have all the fucking mirrors in the world, and it wouldn't be herself she'd harm. No. There are some bitches like that. And then there are the other kind—it's always their own selves they go for. Like this one woman Catherine told me about, sneaked her compact in—but she didn't go for her wrists but for her cunt—cut it all to shreds. Some bitches . . .

———

It hasn't been but a week since Ernest has taken her out of the hospital in Milan and brought her here to Ibiza. I got his post-card when I was traveling in Brazil. In the old days I used to stop everything and come running. Now I come, but I take my own time, and when I get where they are I don't even ask what happened. I used to make it a little ritual of asking: "Catherine, what happened?" "I've just tried to kill my husband."

Now I don't ask, and all the asylums smell the same, like cel-lophane and orange juice. All stone and glass. This time she had to go all the way across the fucking Atlantic to go crazy. Cather-ine had just won this international Italian art prize too—I forget the name of it, but a real prestigious one; and they'd traveled to Milan for her to claim it. She claimed it all right, the bucks and this brass and gold trophy. It's the trophy she tried to do her thing with.

Anyway, well, I remember this one time she'd just tried to kill him, and I got there and there they were sitting on a bench in the hallway outside the locked door, and he was holding her elbow. You'd think they were turtledoves. Baby! If all lovers could look that way! Well, it takes all kinds. And Catherine's got enough jabber to fill the whole country. She starts talking about elbows! Just tried to kill the man and talking about elbows.

"You know, you can tell the age of somebody by the skin on the elbows," she jabbers.

"No. I didn't know that."

Ernest glances up, notices me there before Catherine does. The wrinkles in his forehead seem to peel off, then they deepen. When Catherine notices, she winks at me and keeps on talking.

"Yeah. Pinch the skin up and if it goes back down you're young! Pinch the skin up and if it stays up, you're old."

She tested us.

"We're all old, kiddo!" she chirped.

Naughty Catherine pointed at me. "She wants me to test your pecker!" she exclaimed.

"Stop it," he demanded.

Catherine's little finger, still raised at me, wiggles, then drops to pat her knee.

When the doctor came, Catherine, wearing a clown's grin, disappeared behind the locked door.

Ernest and I gave each other bewildered stares, then he reached into his valise for the doctor's reports.

2

I've got to tell you more about that woman—the one who cut her cunt to threads. I actually saw that broad, before I knew her story. You know how you see people and then learn their story? Then go about wishing you'd first seen them when you knew the shit—all those good things you'd have noticed that you missed. Well, anyway, in fact I'd been sitting on a bench in the hall right beside that woman. It was one of those times when Catherine was "on retreat" in the local "nuttery" (that's her expression), during the years when I'd rush to her. She was in a session with her shrink (nutcracker?) and I had to wait in the hall for her. I could tell the woman was a patient because she was wearing this gray housecoat and silver-colored slippers. She sat there not saying anything, just wringing her hands—just moving one hand in and out and around the other. Finally, the nurse came and told me that Catherine was back in her room.

"I saw you sitting out there with Gwendola."

"Gondola," I'd thought she'd said at first.

Catherine kept shaking her head. "Some species of womankind."

"What?"

She was sitting on her bed with her back against the wall. I sat in the uncomfortable visitor's chair.

"What some species of womankind will do. And that's an intelligent woman too. There are a lot of intelligent people in here. Nuts, but intelligent."

"What'd she do?"

She scratched her knee, reached back and scratched her behind, then scratched inside her ear.

"You know I told you about the compacts?"

"Yeah."

"Well, that darling managed to sneak a compact in here. She had one of her aunts who I swear should be in here herself sneak her in a compact in the bottom of an Easter basket. Some fool examined the chocolate bunnies and shit and forgot to look under the grass, and that's the first thing you do when you check an Easter basket is look under the grass! Anyway, when Gwendola got her compact, she started going to town."

"Cut her wrists?"

"No. Straight for the cunt. They saved what they could. Of course they've got to wait till it heals to find out how much they did save. I believe in saving the beaver myself, and sparing the rod too." I shook my head.

She shrugged. "But from what I hear she'll be lucky if she's still got a hole."

I said nothing. I tried to remember what I hadn't noticed.

"It's sort of funny, you know. All the women nuts sort of like having her around. We don't bother her and she don't bother us, but we sort of just like knowing she's around. The men nuts, on the other hand, don't want to know she's here at all."

Out in the hall, Gwendola had disappeared, but she left the slippers. The only time I've seen her again is in my dreams. Introduce you to her when I see her.

3

I should introduce myself too. My name's Amanda Wordlaw. Wonderful name for a writer, isn't it? Not just my pen name either; it's the name of the man I married. I write fiction. Anyway, I used to. Mostly erotic novels, like those rambling, underground Victorian sex novels. Maybe some of the titles you're familiar with: *Rainbow Stories, The Other Broad's Story, Don't Let Cowgirls Fool Ya'*? Anyway, someone wrote me up in this magazine article: "The Little Horny Bitches Have Come of Age." It was a trashy article, like the kind you'd expect to read if *The Naked Lunch* had been written by a woman. Yet, that's when I stopped writing erotic fiction and started writing travel books: *Fun and Sun in Mexico, Is Paris Really Cleveland?, The Flower Sellers of Madagascar, The Healers of Bahia.*

I guess I'm sort of a choice companion for the Shugers—professional watcher and listener that I am. People who know the Shugers' story—or think they know it—wonder why I stay around them. I don't know why I stay. I could try to come up with a motive, some cliche like "Catherine is the only one who accepts me without question." It's not true. She's wary of me; Ernest is too. They're wary of me, but they take me in too. It's like they need someone else to witness the shit, the spectacle they make of themselves . . . a private spectacle. Catherine has never tried to harm him in public. Even that time on the street in Detroit, as you know, it was a Sunday and the salvage dump was closed; no one else on the backstreet, and the bicycle spoke sticking out between the crevices of the wire fence. And if you have this picture of Catherine receiving her art trophy and then turning suddenly on some stage in Milan, trying to batter Ernest, and then being straitjacketed and carried off, that's not true either. She waited until they were quietly back at the hotel, still radiant in the splendor of the evening, and Ernest loving and proud of her and forgetful that brass and gold were dangerous.

So the attempts at harm are never public, always some careless, sudden private moment. There's publicity abounding, though, rumors of the problem, tall tales of it, a mess of gossip.

Catherine's aura is yellow. That's what this spiritualist, a medium, told us once—this woman who advertised herself as "the grand, international African-American Medium"—and Catherine wouldn't rest until we went. Yellow's supposed to be a good aura, she said. And me? She wouldn't tell me what my aura was, like it frightened her or something. Instead she started telling me about problems I could see already about myself. For instance, I've got eczema on my back and shoulders. She told me about it. Who needs to be told unless she could also cure it? But she wouldn't. Just said it was here. And also I'm an aspirin addict, though I try to limit myself to three of the little buggers a day. Tell me something that can be remedied, I said. But she just laughed, and asked Catherine to hold out her palm so she could see her love line.

Tell us how to keep Catherine from her murderous ambushes.

Here on Ibiza, Ernest has made a temporary solution. He spends only his days with us and at night returns to a hotel on the other side of the island, leaving Catherine and me in the fisherman's house. Don't ask me if they make love in the daytime; that's not my territory. I will say I've never heard lovemaking going on. There are some naughty rumors out about the three of us, though, and I'm defensive about that.

One thing I can say about Ibiza is that it's been a whole month and Catherine has not attempted murder. And on the beach, you sit and feel like you've become the sun.

I like the beaches, but Catherine likes what she calls the "donkey paths," the little narrow streets and tightly packed white-washed buildings. "We first discovered Ibiza on a travel film," Catherine told me. "Can you believe it? Just these marvelous views from the plane, one of those aero-photographers—Ern did an article on one once. I can always tell if I'll like a place if it's got a nice view from the plane. If it makes you think, Wow, let's land there and have a look around! It reminded me of Athens but it reminded Ern of Morocco. I mean, what can beat Athens and Morocco together? Of course Ernest didn't believe it would be as good as the film, but I did. You just can't have an airplane view like that and it not be."

She leans toward me and wiggles her nose (she can do that): "Enough beaches for you, Baby?"

"Yes."

" 'Course I likes the donkey paths myself. Let's go exploring."

'Course it's easy to guess what Ernest likes best about Ibiza: the rest, or is that respite?

(breathing space)

"Are you sleeping with him?" Catherine asked me once, like she'd started herself to believe the rumors, or invent her own.

"No," I said.

She didn't ask anymore, but underlying everything, I think there's still that wonder. This is the truth: Where Ernest is concerned, I keep my hands to myself. He's not interested in me anyway. He's Catherine's—I mean, the shit he puts up with to stay with her, he'd have to be hers, wouldn't he?

You can't control the shit you dream though. Once I dreamed I was standing out on the terrace, and he came up behind me and pulled my skirt up.

" 'Don't let cowboys fool ya'?" he said.

"That's not my story; that's the other broad's story," I said. "I'm better than that."

"Catherine doesn't have to know."

He pulled my panties down.

"Do you like my floppy disk?"

"I don't want her directing any of her harm toward me."

"Coward."

"Don't let cowards fool ya."

"I love you."

"No, you don't; you love Catherine. Go in there and tell her; don't be a shithead."

"Tell me you love me too."

"I can't tell you I love you. I haven't been through enough shit with you to tell you that. You've been through too much shit with Catherine not to love her."

"Call me your love."

"I'll call you my friend, lover."

He fucks me while I hold onto the white, stone rails.

Like I said, you can't control the shit you dream.

"Don't sit under the apple tree with anyone else but me, anyone else but me."

"Let him alone; he's *my* dream man," says Catherine.

Then she is watching, a toothpick stuck in her jaw.

Next thing we're in the bedroom and I'm the one with the toothpick stuck in my jaw and watching.

"Sit under my apple tree," sings Catherine.

Now she's spreadeagled on the bed. Now she pulls off her champagne-colored Danskin bra and Lady Jockey drawers.

"No, you sit under mine," he says.

So he's sitting on the edge of the bed, and Catherine's giving him head. So I'm standing in the door picking my teeth and watching.

"Aren't you afraid?" I ask.

Catherine turns her head and grins at me; she's all teeth. Then she turns back, head dancing between his legs.

"I mean because she's all teeth."

"No, I'm not afraid. She's well-bred."

"Want some?" Catherine asks.

"No," I say.

"Come on, let's eat him up."

"No thanks."

"You know you can tell a man's age by the number of rings around his cock. Look at all these grooves! He's old, kiddo."

She makes those slurping noises like you read in those erotic comix. He rubs the top of her head, strokes it; beads of sweat on the back of her neck, in the corners of his eyebrows. James Brown in the background singing, "It's a man's world . . . uhn uhn uhn.

"You ought to try some, better than a toothpick," Catherine says, holding it delicately between her thumb and little finger. She licks the very tip of it, then she rises.

"You see, there wasn't anything to fear," says Ernest.

"Now me," says Catherine, spread like an eagle on the white quilt. The hairs on her are red. The lips seem longer than normal. They flap like butterflies' wings. They're bronze-pink, but the tips look like they've been dipped in salt.

"Now me," she repeats.

"I'm no eater," says Ernest, folding his arms.

"You see how they are," says Catherine, rising up on her elbows.

I'm sitting on the floor now, and it looks like she's staring at me up from a hill of red fern.

"How are they?"

"You know, how they like to make a cocksucker out of a woman, and then they won't return the favor."

I stare at her, flapping like she's ready to take off.

"Yeah, I know what you mean."

She bends over like a contortionist, slides her own tongue in.

When her head pops up, she's teeth again. She looks like she's advertising them, as my aunt once said of a local dentist.

"What if I Gwendola'd it? Put it on a platter for you, with sprigs of parsley, lemon, pimento, Worcestershire, Louisiana hot sauce?"

"Who's Gwendola?" he asks, matter-of-factly.

"You'd better be glad I'm not Gwendola, Mister."

"So who is she?"

"That's for us girlies to know, and you to be grateful you don't."

Ernest, his arms still folded, looks like he's blowing bubbles. I get into his view so he can blow one toward me.

"Here it is. Come and get it y'all! Join the feast!"

Haven't you had dreams too where you're afraid to look?

4

"I want stuffed grape leaves," Catherine announced as soon as we sat down. "I haven't had stuffed grape leaves in ages. I love 'em."

"You?" Ernest asked. He sat across from us. He was still holding the jacket like a shield, then he laid it on the seat beside him.

"I'll try the grape leaves," I said. "I've never had them."

"They are the most delicious things in the world," said Catherine.

"I'll have the chicken wings with green pepper," said Ernest.

"You always have chicken wings. You don't have anything but chicken wings."

"You always have grape leaves."

"Yes, but Greektown's the only place I can get stuffed grape leaves. You can have chicken anywhere. You don't have to go out on the town to have chicken."

When the waiter came, Ernest ordered a Greek wine, his chicken, and the grape leaves.

"What do you think?" Catherine asked when I bit into the stuffed leaves. I chewed. Really, it looked a little like stuffed cabbage but had a taste I couldn't exactly place.

"I like it," I said.

"It's just too good. How's your chicken, Baby?"

"Very good."

"You can have chicken anywhere."

"They use different spices," Ernest defended.

"I don't care how it's spiced, chicken's still a bore," said Catherine. "You can kill me with boredom. Nothing kills me like boredom."

We said nothing. Catherine glanced around the room. "Looky y'all, there's a Chinaman eating Greek. I read somewhere where you shouldn't call a Chinaman a Chinaman. It's considered derogatory. It doesn't sound derogatory to me."

"That's because you're not Chinese," said Ernest.

"Look, there's a Chinese gentleman eating Greek. Is that what I should say?"

"I guess so," said Ernest.

"That sounds derogatory to me," said Catherine. "I'd rather be a Chinaman than a Chinese gentleman any day."

"That's because you're not Chinese."

"Should I go over and ask him what he prefers to be called?"

"No, Catherine."

"What am I? I mean, if Amanda wasn't here with her sweet bothered and bewildered self, and they were looking at this anonymous Black couple, you and me, what would I be? They'd say, 'Looky, there's a Black gentleman eating Greek and there's . . .' What would they say?"

She turned sideways and looked in the mirror that ran along the wall. Her expression changed; she tried to look dangerous. "Here, she is, folks, everybody's evil Black bitch."

"Hush."

"Don't I look like everybody's evil Black bitch to you?"

"No, you look like Tweety Bird," I said.

"You're not here, remember," she said, glancing my way, but not looking at me. "They'd say, 'There's that Black gentleman and there's his evil Black bitch.'"

"I thought you were 'everybody's,'" I put in.

"You're not here."

"To be honest, Catherine, it doesn't interest me in the least what they'd say," said Ernest.

Her face fell. She stared at my plate. "If you're not going to eat your grape leaves, I'll finish them."

"I'm not here, remember," I said.

She said nothing. Finally, I exchanged plates with her. She ate.

"You know, Ernest wrote this article, which when you get down to the nitty-gritty said essentially 'You are what you eat.' From what the article said, it seems like the Orientals are really the only people who eat *right*, like when they start eating Western food, that really screws them up. After he wrote that article, we started to go by the foods it recommended. I got bored stiff after a week. He was bored too, but he pretended like he wasn't. You know, he'd written this article, so he felt he had to practice what he preached. I was bored silly. Are we still going tomorrow to get my rubber stuff?"

"You gave up your chance for your rubber stuff."

"I know where there's a place where there's nothing but rubber stuff. They melt rubber or something, so all they have is this rubber stuff, just everything. We can go there."

"Gave up your chance for your rubber stuff." He was teasing now. "Yeah, you can have your rubber stuff. The way things have gotten, though, it looks like we'll have to rent an apartment just for the odds and ends."

Either Catherine glanced at me like I was one of the odds and ends, or I imagined it.

"I knew you couldn't say no to Tweety Bird," said Catherine.

"How do you know it's Tweety Bird I'm not saying no to," said Ernest, with a sly smile.

Catherine gave him his sly smile back, then she bent down suddenly, licked her plate, popped her head up. Just then the waiter was there to take our plates. Her sly smile fell on him.

"Do the Greeks eat Chinese?" she asked, peeking up.

Outside, Catherine patted her stomach. We strolled.

"That was a nice *repast*," she said. "Have you got any chewing gum?"

"How come I'm always here when you want something?" I asked, reaching in my purse for some spearmint.

"I don't know; why are you?"

I gave her the gum. She giggled and ran ahead of us. The socks on one of her feet had made its way down inside her shoe. She disappeared around a corner.

"I'll go ahead," I suggested.

Ernest shook his head.

We walked on.

Catherine came back around the corner, strolling, chewing her gum, smacking it rather, looking like she didn't know us. She passed us, tipped an imaginary hat. "How do?"

We turned, waited for her. She about-faced and joined us, running.

"Is that y'all?" She peered like a little old woman who'd forgotten her specs. "I didn't know that was y'all. I thought that was everybody's Black gentleman and his lady, but that really is y'all, ain't it?"

"Who are we?" I asked.

Ernest just stood.

"I ain't telling. You won't get it from me. Beat me with a rubber hose and I won't tell."

"Even Tweety Bird gets uhn-uhn today," said Ernest. "No rubber stuff."

"Not even a band?"

"Not even a band."

"How do you expect me to work if you keep limiting my materials?"

"You limit your own materials," he said. He walked.

"Come and see the new Catherine Shuger exhibition, folks. Catherine Shuger, the only sculptress to work with chocolate pudding and a spoon!"

"It's been done," I said.

"Has it?" Catherine stood there looking like she really thought it had been.

"Come along," said Ernest.

We followed him like chickens.

5

Stay clear of salvage dumps and rubber factories.

6

In Catherine's sculpture studio, music is always playing, mostly jazz—Satchmo, Miles, Tyner, the great Trane. Sometimes, though, she'll play opera—*Carmen, La Bohème, Le Nozze di Figaro, Pagliacci, Orfeo ed Euridice, Tannhäuser, The Magic Flute*. Now, as I enter, Miles's *Bitches Brew* flies from the speakers and she's standing at her worktable, gluing wooden feathers on a piece called *The Birdcatcher*, made of bits of wood and aluminum and found objects, a piece she keeps dismantling and rearranging, a piece she's been working on, on and off, for years, like that fellow's puzzle sculpture, except the artist herself can't decide what piece to put where and keep it.

I sit on a pallet that she has for me in the corner of the room. I sit with my knees raised, my arms on my knees and my chin in my hands. I don't disturb her while she wrinkles her forehead. I sit like a stone cat and watch.

"Do you still have that war penny?" she asks, over her shoulder.

"Yeah."

I fish for it in the pockets of my culottes, start to rise.

"Toss it."

She catches it.

It's a gray penny, made during the war when they were out of copper. We're both war babies.

"I'll find some place for it," she says, putting it on the corner of the table with other found objects—shells, rubber bands, shards of who knows what.

"That looks good," I say. "I like that one."

"No, it's not right; it's still not right."

"I don't think you ever want to finish it."

I think she likes destroying and recreating it. I think she'd like to go on forever.

"It's not right."

It's not right: You're not supposed to take communion unless you're right, they say in the Jehovah's Witnesses church I grew up in. So no one ever takes it because no one's ever right. Except sometimes a real old man or a real old woman will take it. I couldn't believe that all you had to do was get old to get right.

When I was in Brazil, Catherine wrote me a letter: "I miss you, old girl. I miss seeing your smiling face. We're living on the white-washed island of Ibiza, land of expatriates, of mirages, of fortresses. Come stay with us."

My face is not always smiling, but whenever she asks me to come stay with them, I come. Sometimes I come frowning, wondering what new shit Catherine will pull.

Ernest says my presence makes Catherine happy, but Catherine always reminds me of de Kooning's *Woman and Bicycle*; you never know where the real smile is supposed to be; smile = laughing teeth.

"What would we do without you," Catherine says as I arrive.

Ernest kisses my jaw and there's Catherine standing in the door wearing a yellow dress. Ever since that medium told her that her aura was yellow, she's worn yellow. She smiles at me and I smile back, then go give her a kiss too.

"Did you have a good time in Brazil?" she asks. "Did you enjoy yourself?"

"Yeah."

"Meet anyone special?"

"No."

"Sure you did."

"You look like a canary."

"But you wouldn't tell us, would you?"

Her brown nose contains two freckles and a mole.

She hugs me and stands close to my face. I back away like I always do, to keep at least some of my own territory.

"Do you know how happy you make me?"

I follow her into the house.

Today I notice gray in Catherine's hair. She reaches up and brushes sweat from her forehead. She has gray sideburns, edges.

Ernest peeks his head in the door of Catherine's studio.

"Oh, you're working." He comes inside, stands watching Catherine a moment. "You're still on that wretched thing? Every one looks the same to me. Why don't you move onto something else? That's just holding you back, it seems to me. Move on to something else."

"You used to say I was too impatient, rushing to the next thing."

"Well, there's a mean, Baby; there's such a thing as a mean."

She looks at him like she's the mean baby.

"I want to get it," mumbles Catherine.

"Suit yourself."

He turns to me. I look at the mole on his cheek, then his playful brown eyes.

"Manda, what are you doing, Babe? Nothing? Come out and talk to me."

He grabs my hand and pulls me up. Catherine glances toward us, mumbles something, goes on with her assembling.

"So how are you?" he asks as we go outside.

"Okay."

He still holds my hand. A vein shaped like a Y on the back of his hand jumps up. When he lets go of my hand the vein relaxes. I stare at the labyrinth of blue veins against his ruddy brown skin. There's a mole on the back of his hand too.

He pulls his lounge chair up next to mine. What do we stare out at? Must be blue sky. Blue as his veins? When he grabs the arm of the chair, the Y shoots up again. Y=?

"Brazil treat you good? Must have. You look good. What were you doing there anyway?"

"Research."

"New novel?"

"No, another travel book. Actually, a guide to the medicinal plants of the area."

"Sounds interesting."

"I want her to talk about the fellow she met." Catherine enters sulking. "She never talks about her new fellows."

"I told you I didn't meet anyone special."

"You're a liar. You're glowing. You can't glow unless you're in love. Isn't she glowing, Ern?"

"Like a glowworm."

"Who'd you meet?"

Ernest is standing behind Catherine, his hand on her shoulders.

"I've got to go," he's saying.

"You just got here."

"I know, but I've been all day on that laser piece. I'm exhausted."

"You're spoiling things."

"I'll have breakfast with you girls tomorrow."

"Manda's here to protect you; you don't have to be afraid of the dark."

Ernest frowns, glances at me. My forehead feels like it's made out of butter.

Catherine pouts, turns suddenly, kisses him. He disappears behind her head.

When his face appears again, his bottom lip is bleeding.

"I'll get some peroxide," I say, getting up from the chaise lounge.

"No," he says.

"I'll get some peroxide," I repeat.

He starts past me. I grab his hand, reach into my pocket, take the cotton from an aspirin bottle, stand up and wipe his lip.

"Are you still taking that shit?" he asks, pointing to the aspirin.

"Yeah."

"I thought you'd quit that shit. But you're a grown woman. What can I tell you? You're grown up."

I dab his lip with the cotton.

When he leaves, I turn to stare at Catherine. I don't have any more whys for her; I just stare and she stares.

"I'm going to fix dinner," I say finally.

"He didn't even stay for dinner. He could have stayed for dinner. Maybe he's just afraid of the dark." She sucks at her teeth, then says singsong, "Maybe he's just afraid of me."

"Is that what you like? A man to fear you?"

"You like it," she says. "Every woman likes it. That cunt-shredder liked it. Doesn't that sound just like the name of an appliance?"

We have no real knives, only plastic ones. We have plastic forks. Only the spoons are real. In the kitchen I make a chicken stew and jello with pineapple slices. Oyster crackers sit on a Chinet paper plate.

Catherine, at the table, looks like a magpie.

"Smells good."

"He could have stayed to keep *you* company," she says, "even if he's had enough of me."

"If he had stayed, you'd have driven him out. You'd have found some way."

I spoon stew into plastic bowls, place her bowl before her, sit down with mine.

"He always brings you to some lovely place, and you start acting like a fool again. Even I'm embarrassed for him, and you know it takes a lot of shit to embarrass me. I think you want to go back."

"I'm no Gwendola."

"We're all Gwendolas, one way or the other."

"I'm not that brave."

"I don't call it brave."

"Well, not even the honey badger goes for its own."

Remember Robert Ruark? Remember *The Honey Badger*? Catherine gave me that book to read when she learned my story, or thought she'd learned it. His description of women. They're (We're) like the honey badger—they (we?) go straight for a man's groin. Of course at the time I just asked, "What?"

She stares into her bowl.

"You know I don't want to go back."

"I don't know."

She sniffs at the stew.

"Did you know human bites could kill?" she asks.

"Yeah, I know."

"You know?"

"Don't worry; your bite won't kill him."

"I can't stop."

"The hell you can't! You've got a fucking soul, don't you? You've got a fucking *will*? You're a fucking human being, aren't you?"

She sniffs at the stew again, then takes up a spoonful.

She swallows, then purses her lips together.

"Yeah, I'm a fucking human being. What did you mean when you said that erotic perversion was the negative side of love?"

"When did I say that?"

"One of your characters said it."

"I can't remember what my characters say."

"What did you mean? I kept reading it over and I couldn't make out what you meant."

"You, kiddo. You're one weird bitch."

She looks frightened. Her eyelids thicken. The space between them jumps together.

"No, I'm kidding. I'm just kidding. To tell the truth I don't the fuck know what the fuck I meant. To tell the truth."

She rubs her upper lip, hair at the corner of her lip bleached light brown; she rubs at the hair like she's trying to erode it.

"Try electrolysis," I say.

7

Speaking of weird bitches, there's this woman Catherine knows, this white woman she went to art school with, or some shit. No, she met her at one of those artists' colonies. They take writers up there too, but I've never applied. You're supposed to go there and work. I can't get shit done around other writers. I can drink, but I can't write. I can drink myself under the fucking table.

But anyway, I met this one weird bitch when I went with Catherine to Toledo because they were showing some of Catherine's work at the Toledo Art Museum and she wanted to also go see this woman. The woman was supposed to—about ten years ago—have been a big deal in the New York art world; people were claiming she was the new female *Dali* or some big shit like that, only more erotic.

Anyway, we get there, and this bitch is living in a fucking trailer—a rusty trailer—and's got this daughter who looks like a sick elf—short with blonde hair and toothpick arms and legs; pixie ears—and the woman, who Catherine said was some great beauty, she's gone to pot and got stringy, dishwater blonde hair— *grasses* hair, like the French word for dishwater and grease is the same thing. I've seen an old picture of her, though, and you couldn't say she wasn't a good-looking broad and like I say about ten years ago she was this big cheese in New York.

But what was funny was the way she treated her kid. What was it she called her? Let me try to recreate the scene.

First this weird bitch looks kind of upset because Catherine didn't come by herself but brought this stranger with hiking boots along, but she invites us into the trailer anyway. Now it's bigger inside than it looked outside. It's really a nice little apartment, comfortable looking, tastefully decorated like a magazine ad out of the fifties.

We go into the living room. The kid is in there eating popcorn, sitting on the floor, with her head against a leather armchair. Yeah. No, chocolate bonbons out of a plastic Glad bag. Like a pixie, but a wilted one.

Anyway, I didn't say shit. I just sat there. The kid kept looking at me though. Pig? No. Hog? Yeah. That was what she called her.

"Tatum, you hog," was the first thing this woman said. "Give me that chocolate."

She took it, put it in the refrigerator, came back and sat in the chair, and Catherine and I sat on the couch, and the kid sat on the floor between her mother's legs.

"It's really good to see you, Cathy. I saw your show. It was wonderful."

"Why didn't you come to the opening?"

"Well, I couldn't get away. They tie you down, you know. I work for this trucking company."

"You drive a truck?"

"No." She laughs. "I write up invoices."

"Mommy, I want some popcorn."

"Tatum, you hog, you just had chocolate."

"I want popcorn." Tatum beat on her mother's knees with little white fists. "Popcorn!"

By the way, this woman's name is Gillette, can you believe it? Like she was named after the fucking razor blade.

"Here you go, darling."

She reached in a drawer on a table beside the chair and took out a cellophane bag of popcorn. She tossed it to her. "Hog."

Then she introduced the girl.

"This is Sister, my daughter."

She held the back of the child's neck, then pinched at her hair. The child had green, slanting eyes. Almost Japanese eyes, except she was as pale as Midol. I kept my distance, but Catherine made her way over to her.

"I thought I'd find you living in New York, then someone told me you were living here!" Catherine said.

"Uh, I still go to New York for occasional shows. But I don't work in a rush the way I used to."

"But a grand rush," Catherine exclaimed.

"Well, I felt so harried . . . is harried the word? No, bedeviled. I just had to get it all out."

"Some great stuff," Catherine explained to me.

I stared at the woman's pale thighs spreading into the brown leather of the chair. She was wearing short-shorts. I could feel leather sticking to my own thighs and the sting when one rose.

"I have to support the kid you see, but it still gives some time to paint. Not like in the old days."

"I paint too," said the kid.

"I've started her on watercolors. Uh, she's very good. Better than I was at her age. Can I show them one of your watercolors?"

Tatum rolled her eyes to the ceiling. "Uhn-uhn."

"She's certainly not like I was," said Gillette. "I'd corner everybody who came to our house, showing them my stuff, and I wasn't nearly so good as she is. To tell the truth, I wasn't very good at all, but everybody would pat me on the head anyway and tell me 'How nice.' I wasn't good at all, but I thought I was. I don't know whether Tatum has that conceit or not, because you never know what in the world she's thinking." She stared at Tatum for a minute, but you couldn't read what she was thinking.

"Instead of selling lemonade I used to set up my paintings in the neighborhood, pretend I was in Montmartre or on St. Germain Boulevard. I was the little darling. I thought I was good because people would come and buy my little paintings. But there was this horrible man, though, who said something perfectly awful to me. He said, 'You're an interesting little girl, but your work's not very good. They're buying your work because you're an interesting little girl.' He said either 'interesting' or 'nice' or 'pretty'—one of those bland adjectives. I thought it was the most awful thing to say. But of course it wasn't an awful thing at all. Because if he hadn't said that I wouldn't have got good. I went to work then. I wanted to be able to do anything in painting."

"Anything," Tatum said.

"Can I just show them one little watercolor?"

"Uhn-uhn."

"She's not like I was."

Gillette was braless in a white T-shirt and those short-short cut-off jeans. The little girl was wearing a straw cowboy hat and had little red pimples on her forehead, which it seemed she was too young to be getting. But it was probably from candy and buttery popcorn. She looked about seven.

"She's great, isn't she?" or "What did you think of Gillette?" Catherine will ask when we're on the plane heading back.

"Not much," I'll say, or I'll try to please her and say, "Yeah, she's something."

"It's roomier in here than I thought it would be," Catherine said. "Than it looks from the outside, I mean."

"Yes, it is. It's nice, roomy enough. But I really don't have room enough for my paintings though. A friend lets me store them in her basement."

"They shouldn't be in a basement!" Catherine exclaimed.

"Oh, you should see the stuff I do now. You wouldn't recognize it. . . . I bet you were surprised to see I'd *reproduced*, too, the way I used to talk about being the lone wolf devoted to nothing but her art."

"What's reproduced?" asked the kid.

"*You*," said Gillette.

"I'm Reproduced. . . . I want some peanuts."

"You've got popcorn."

The little girl hands the popcorn back to her. "Where's my peanuts?"

Gillette reaches in the drawer of the end table, puts the popcorn bag back, takes out a cellophane bag of peanuts. "You little hog, what do you say?"

"Thank you, ma'am."

The kid begins stuffing peanuts in her mouth.

Gillette pinches her shoulder. "Tatum, don't try to put all of those in your mouth at one time. Don't chew with your mouth open. Hog. Ladies don't eat like that. Eat one at a time. Eat like a lady."

Tatum continues to eat with her mouth open.

"She lost her toy monkey and she's been impossible."

"I didn't lost it; you threw it away," says the kid.

"You lost it. When we moved. You were responsible for the whereabouts of your own things; you know that."

"You threw it away." Splinters of peanuts escape from her pouting lips.

"Don't talk with your mouth open, that's impolite."

Tatum keeps munching, then she shakes the empty bag.

"They're all gone now," Gillette says and picks the child up, sits her in her lap, and shoves the child's head against her breasts.

"I want peanuts." Tatum shakes her head, wrinkles her nose, and pops away. "You stink, lady."

Gillette looks embarrassed, puts her palm against the side of Tatum's face and pushes her head back against her breasts.

"I want peanuts," Tatum says again.

"You hog, you ate them up; they're all gone. I'm sorry, do you two want some beer or something? Beer's all I've got."

"No, thanks," says Catherine.

"I'll take some," I say.

She puts Tatum down, goes to the refrigerator, and brings back a can of Blatz.

"Uh, do you want a glass?" she asks.

"Naw, this is fine."

"Why did you throw away my monkey?" Tatum asks when Gillette sits back down.

"I didn't throw away your monkey, Sister. Anyway, you were responsible. I can't keep up with your things and mine too."

"Yes, you did too. You threw it away."

Gillette puts her hand over Tatum's mouth.

"You see how they are?" she says. "Are you going to be quiet, Sister?"

Tatum nods.

Gillette takes her hand away. "Tell me yes."

"Yes," says Tatum.

Gillette takes a deep breath, blows it in Tatum's face. Tatum giggles, then she pinches her nose.

8

When I was seven I tried to take something off the communion plate. My mother pushed my hand away but didn't explain why. I'd seen this real old woman take some wine and crackers and I'd wanted some too. Then when I went down in the basement to use the bathroom this biggish girl stood in front of the bathroom door with her hands on her hips like she was guarding the toilet.

"Didn't anybody ever tell you you're not supposed to take communion unless you're right?"

"Yeah," I lied. "I know what banal means too."

I always added that whenever anyone questioned my age or my knowledge. Either "banal" or some other new word I'd picked up.

"Then why'd you reach your hand in the communion plate? You ain't right."

"I'm as right as that old woman."

"No, because she's too old to do anything wrong. And you just starting to do yours."

"Let me go in the bathroom."

"Look at you, ain't big as a minute and think you're right."

"I got a right to go pee."

"I bet you think you got a right to do everything, don't you? Look at you."

"Let me in the bathroom. I know I got a right to pee."

"Look at you."

Finally, she moved out of my way.

When I passed her, she whispered, "Banal? I bet you don't even know the difference between *right* and *right*."

9

Gillette comes back into the room. She's pinned her hair back in a ponytail. High full cheeks, dotted with a touch of rouge. Her rounded chin is as babyish as Tatum's. Her nose looks powdered, but the rest is as shiny as if she's just stepped out of a Turkish bath.

"You guys ready?"

We go to Hardee's and eat roast beef sandwiches. Gillette and Tatum sit in the booth across from Catherine and me.

"Do you like it, Sister? Is it good?" Gillette asks.

"Yes," says Tatum.

Gillette wipes barbecue sauce from the corner of Tatum's mouth.

"Take little bites," she warns.

Tatum keeps her mouth open, smacks and chews, makes it her little rebellion.

"I guess you can see how it is," says Gillette.

Catherine nods. Gillette glances at me a moment, then bites into her roast beef. The roast beef is tough and sticks between my front teeth.

"You did get married though. I'm just noticing your ring," she says to Catherine.

"Yes."

"Is he a nice man?"

"Yes, very nice."

"I bet he's nice."

I brush my tongue across the front of my teeth, but the roast beef won't bulge.

Gillette pushes a loose strand of hair back behind her ear, scratches her jaw. Her nostrils flare a bit.

"I read about one of your shows, the one in Montreal. You're doing really swell, kid. I did like what I saw here. You must have a lot of *time*. I really envy your *time*. I envy your time more than your man. My marriage didn't stick. I guess you can see that. The moving I was talking about was us clearing out."

"Clearing out," Tatum echoes.

"I don't have as much time as when we were at the colony," Catherine says.

"Nobody does." Gillette frowns. Her shoulders rise till they almost touch her ears. "I don't like to think about those good days. They were too good, weren't they?"

Gillette rests her chin on her collar. There are two chins. When she raises her head again, one of them disappears.

I scrape my teeth with my little finger, capturing roast beef under my nail. I suck at the nail. The kid is looking at me grinning. Barbecue rouge dots her jaws. You could glean roast beef from her front teeth.

Gillette glances around Hardee's, glances at me, swallows beef, pats Tatum's jaws with her napkin. Tatum wriggles, uses her own napkin.

"It's sort of hard to realize that now it's your generation that sucks. I left Tatum with a babysitter and went to this club the other night. I haven't been to a club in ages. All the people were so *young*. They were just so *young*. I was so out of place. But they were *us*, though; they really were us." She looks intensely at Catherine. Catherine watches Tatum. "I can imagine them *us*. But of course none of them could ever imagine they were *me*. Do you sort of know what I mean? I wouldn't even dance. The music was too fast. It's still rock, but it zooms. Or maybe I've just slowed up." She laughs a bit. "They couldn't even imagine they were us."

"I can," says Tatum.

"Tatum, you don't even know what I mean."

Tatum pouts, then she sings Billy Joel's tune, her mouth full of masticated beef, "It's still rock 'n' roll to me."

Gillette puts Tatum to bed, and we grownups go back into the kitchen. As Catherine and I sit down at the table, Gillette reaches behind the refrigerator and pulls out a canvas and a pile of sticks. She arranges the sticks into an easel, places the canvas on it, and begins to work. On top of the refrigerator is her paintbox.

"I hope you girls don't mind," she says, "but this is the only time I have to paint."

"We understand," says Catherine. "Anyway, it'll be good to watch you again. I remember watching you work at the colony."

"Eh, I hate to remember those days."

She makes light brushstrokes on the canvas, a half-done painting that looks like two eyes peeking through trees, growing out of a woman's broad back. Except the back looks like both a woman's back and her cunt, and one of the trees a man's privates, the tree's crown his balls.

"That's great," says Catherine.

"Oh, it used to be simple as pie," says Gillette, "but now it's like I have to strain, you know . . . Eh, can one of you get that bowl of mushrooms out of the refrigerator—the one with 'no' tacked on it?"

Catherine gets it out. "Saving this for us? Something to nibble on while you work?"

"No," exclaims Gillette. "I paint with those—that's to keep Tatum's hands off. She'll eat anything. They make a nice texture, so I use them sometimes instead of brushes. They're poison anyway—they're Amanitas whateveryoucall them—somebody told me what they were called—the scientific name I mean—but I forgot. But the English for them is 'destroying angels.'" She makes a noise I can't describe—something between a sigh and a whinny. "Actually, Tatum influenced me to do this—I mean the *idea* of it. When she was a baby and I gave her her first watercolors, she'd take anything. I mean she'd grab anything and everything and paint with it. I had to watch her all the time. Anything and everything. It just seemed so primitive, and so right. That you really could paint with anything. And then when her dad and I were on this camping trip I just grabbed this handful of mushrooms and said why not? They're really wonderful to paint with. It was her dad who told me what they were, actually. He thought I was just crazy enough to put them in the soup. All mushrooms look alike to me, but that's the first thing they teach you, that some mushrooms are poison and you shouldn't just go grabbing any of them. That's the first thing they teach. But I never would have thought to use anything but a brush if it hadn't been for my baby. So anyway, when I tell him what I intend to do with them, like an experiment, he looks at me like I'm still in playschool. That's the way he is about art. It's a drag. An artist should marry an artist, but then that's a drag too. So what do you do? If I'd pulled a Gauguin, I'd have felt like a louse. So I brought Tatum with me. But what do I win? The rocking horse?"

Catherine hands Gillette the bowl of destroying angels, and Gillette sets it down on a high chair that must have been Tatum's when she was a baby and begins painting—twisting one mushroom after another in a paint dish like a shaving brush and then applying it to the canvas: The mushrooms are so fragile that after a few strokes one breaks, and she discards that in the trashcan and picks up another. They are fragile, but they seem in some places to give a thicker, more full-bodied texture than ordinary brushes; in others a finer, more delicate, almost elusive texture, as if she's hardly touched the canvas.

"That's really great," gushes Catherine.

"Thanks, but I wish I were *growing*, but I don't have time to grow . . . Uh, there's a box of nachos on the table if you guys want to nibble on something . . . or if you'd rather have raisins, something else?"

"No, I like nachos. Will it bother you?"

"No. I could paint through the Blitz. I know a woman who actually did."

Catherine grabs for the box. I shake my head when she asks if I want some. She starts crunching.

"I remember it used to be that anybody's presence in my life was a fuss and a bother. More than a bother, an outrage. I used to feel just that obsessed about my work. I would have killed before letting anyone interfere with it, you know." She glances at me. "I used to have this little saying. 'Never kill your work for a man or a child, kill them first.'" She laughs a bit. "Cathy remembers."

"Yeah," nods Catherine. "I know what you mean."

"No, you don't." Gillette throws one broken mushroom into the trash, picks up another. "You're too good. You wouldn't kill a soul for art; you'd let them kill you first."

Gillette glances at me again.

"No, I wouldn't," mumbles Catherine.

She sniffs at a nacho, pops it into her mouth. She looks sleepy.

"I was a real bitch then," says Gillette softly. "I thought you had to be a bitch to make great art. Like if Picasso had been a woman, he would have been a bitch. Like a woman's a bitch when she makes the same choices a man would make without thinking." She shrugs. "Gauguin." She laughs. "This is as close to Tahiti as we could get . . . I used to be a bitch though."

"You weren't a bitch," says Catherine, chewing a nacho. "You were always nice to me."

Gillette looks at Catherine like you'd look at a child.

"You guys can go to bed when you want to. Sometimes I'm up half the fucking night with this shit."

10

"Uh, what are you into now?" asks Gillette over breakfast.

Tatum dabs her oatmeal like it's fingerpaint.

"Improvisation," says Catherine. "You know, assembling, found objects, that sort of stuff."

"That sounds good," says Gillette, chewing a donut.

Then she says, "That's a little different from the way you used to be, Cathy. I mean, your art always seemed so premeditated. I don't know why I said premeditated. That's hardly the word for art. It's good to know you've gotten freer; you can never get too free, can you? . . . Eat your oatmeal, Baby."

11

Gillette stands looking at me fully for the first time. She'd waited till we're standing at the airport, ready to board the plane, it seems, before she tried to get a good look at me.

"Uh, are you a painter too?" she asks.

"No, she's a writer," says Catherine. "I'm sure you've read something by Amanda Wordlaw. Some really heavy stuff, heavy stuff."

"I'm sorry, but I haven't." Gillette stares at me. "I guess what little time I have I spend with my own work. I haven't done much *reading* in years, of anybody. But I'll try to get something of yours the next chance I get."

"You'll like her. She writes like you paint," says Catherine.

Gillette frowns slightly, then she looks amused.

"Well, it was good to meet you," she says, curtly.

I nod.

"You're welcome to come back anytime," she adds suddenly. "If you're in town. I mean, even if you're without Catherine."

"Okay."

"So long," she tells Catherine. "I always love seeing you."

They hug and give each other little kisses. Catherine kisses Tatum.

I say "Goodbye" to them both, and Catherine and I board the plane.

"She's great, isn't she?" Catherine says when we're settled.

"She's okay."

Catherine pouts. "Well, she likes you anyway."

"I don't see how. I didn't say half a word to her."

"You always have to behave like such a fucker, don't you?"

"Not always," I whisper back, and lean into her ear. "Sometimes I behave like a fuck-ee."

12

"What are you doing?"

"The dishes," I say.

"Come and keep me company."

"No. Let me finish."

"Come and keep me company," she demands.

I follow her into the living room. We sit opposite each other in peacock chairs but do not talk. She eats dried pineapple from a bag, dried bits of pineapple that look like rubber.

"Want some?"

"No. I'm still full from dinner."

"Amanda, you always leave us."

"I can't just spend my days here, Catherine. I have a life, too, you know."

"Yeah, but you never talk about it though." She waits. "That's a hint, kid."

I reach into my pocket and take out the aspirin bottle. I uncap it, fish underneath the cotton, lift one of them out. I no longer hunt for water. I chew and swallow the aspirin like a piece of candy.

"Those little fuckers," she says.

"What?"

"Those little fuckers you take. Why is it that everyone has to have their little fuckers? Something to try to fuck themselves up with?" she asks. "It seems harmless, but even too much aspirin can be toxic. Do you want to get bleeding ulcers or something?

"We know all about them, you see, because Ernest did an article on them, sent me a copy—'The Dangers of Over-the-Counter Medicines'—that had a whole section on aspirin, which he starred.

"Do you want to get acidosis?"

"What are your little fuckers?" I ask, popping the cap back on the aspirin bottle and putting it in my pocket. When I don't take them my head aches and I'm nauseous. Addict's symptoms.

Her seaweed-green eyes. Have you ever seen a brown woman with green eyes? It's wild. She won't answer.

"What are Ernest's little fuckers?" I ask, because I know the answer to that one.

"He's got only one little fucker."

"What?"

"Me."

On the terrace, Catherine rubs my back and shoulders with olive oil. We have just finished breakfast and Ernest is sitting at the table with us, reading a Spanish newspaper.

I have the back of a crocodile. If I don't put oil on it every morning it flakes. In some countries and times, I would have been sacred. They would have called me "crocodile woman." I would have had the back of the crocodile god. But now it's only a nuisance. Now the doctors' only clue to its cause is "nerves": Now there are no keys to some source in a supernatural world. It's a malady, pure and simple. Malaise of spirit?

"What are those?"

Catherine points out the string around my neck.

"Crocodile teeth," I say. "Someone gave them to me when I was in Madagascar. They're for luck. At least in the old days people thought they were lucky." I laugh. "They'd go into battle armed with crocodile teeth and expect to *win*."

She picks at one of the flakes, then oils it.

"Tell us about your Madagascar lover," she says.

Ernest looks up from his newspaper. The sunlight makes his forehead shimmer.

"Don't tell her a thing," he says. "It's your business."

Catherine tosses the bottle of olive oil at him. He ducks. It cracks on the concrete.

I rise to get a broom and dustpan, come back to shovel glass and oil into the metal pan. Catherine stands at my shoulder watching. I work fast so that she won't have the notion to grab a sliver. I make a note to carry my oil in a plastic cosmetic bottle. Some of the slivers are as small as crushed ice.

Ernest is standing at the railing. He has poured himself another cup of coffee and is calmly drinking it. He brushes the hair back from his forehead. Streaks of gray and ochre and black. This is an ordinary morning, his look tries to say.

But Catherine's look. She watches the glass like the proverbial charmed serpent with emeralds for eyes.

In the kitchen, I wrap the glass carefully in brown paper, shove it into the very bottom of the trash can.

When I come back to the terrace, Catherine is alone, sitting at the breakfast table.

"Where did Ernest disappear to?"

"Gone to the beach for a swim," she says matter-of-factly.

"I wonder when he'll ever get enough of you," I can't help but say.

Today I won't tiptoe around her.

First she gives me one of those "What's this?" looks, then she gives me what we've dubbed her movie-star smile, all bright and vacuous.

"He never gets enough of me," she says, speaking slowly and staring over my shoulder. I'm tempted to glance back to see if she's really reading cue cards, but I keep my eyes in hers. "Like I never get enough of him. But you, 'you little horny bitch,' you wouldn't know anything about never getting enough of one man. Tell me about your lovers."

"I think I'll join Ernest in that swim."

"Only the swim, girlie."

Now she's looking at me. Now she's not the movie star. Now she's the witch in the comic book. Now she's the wicked witch in *The Wizard of Oz*.

"I'll think about it. But you know how we little horny bitches are!"

She looks around for something to throw at me, and finding nothing, settles down, leans her lion's head back, and catches the sun in her face.

Her forehead doesn't shimmer; it glows.

13

Ernest isn't in the water. He still has on his street clothes and is simply sitting in the sand, his arms around his knees, what I call my stone cat position, because I'd once seen a stone cat in a museum that some ancient Egyptian sculptor had fashioned and it looked exactly like me when I sat like that. I don't say anything to him. I just sit down beside him and become a stone cat too. He doesn't glance at me but seems to know all the same who's there.

We stare out at the sea, the sky, the bathers, the little boats. It's like sitting in the middle of a postcard.

"You're always bringing Catherine to postcard places," I observe.

"What?"

"This looks exactly like a postcard, doesn't it? Like we're sitting in the middle of a postcard."

"Yes," he mumbles.

"Sky as blue as horseshoe crab's blood. That sounds awful, doesn't it? I got that from one of your articles though."

"Did you?"

"The one on marine animals. You described how blue the horseshoe crab's blood is."

"It's really bluer than that," he says.

"Are you bluer than that?"

He glances at me. "Let's walk."

We leave the beach and enter one of the donkey paths.

"I didn't know you read my articles," he says.

"Catherine always clips them and sends them to me."

"Does she?"

"You sent the one you thought would do me some good, but she sends every one of them. She's very proud of you, you know."

He grimaces. He smiles a bit, says nothing. We brace against the wall of a building for a passing auto. I stand pigeon-toed.

Steep stone stairs lead to a promontory, a sort of natural terrace, that looks out onto the beach. We sit down. He strokes his bottom lip.

"I have a world of questions for you myself," he says softly.

"Hazard them," I say.

He throws his head back and gives a long, luxurious laugh.

"Not if you put it that way, I won't."

I watch a saffron-colored sailboat, then another that looks like it has been scoured with sand.

"I guess I'll be heading back," I say.

"Do you want to go somewhere for a drink?"

"I don't think so."

He stands up. I still sit with my back against the rock. He sighs through his teeth.

"Besides I don't want to get too mellow," I say, sounding dryer than I'd intended. "Catherine's in Oz with me again."

We say Catherine is in Oz when she behaves witchy. Catherine has come up with that one herself too. She'd twisted "at odds" into "in Oz" one time, and we'd laughed so hard and liked the expression so much that we were very quickly out of Oz and giggling companions when we explained to Ernest what it meant.

"Catherine's always in Oz," he says.

I stand up.

"Anyway, you're never in Oz with her long," he says. "You've got your little red shoes."

He's looking like he wished he had his.

14

I met Catherine at an artists' conference—not writers, but sculptors, painters, weavers, candlestick makers. I was staying at a hotel in Detroit, because some folks at Wayne State University had invited me to give a fiction reading. When I came back from the reading, I wandered upstairs and discovered some people sitting behind a long table piled with fliers and registration forms. I asked them what was going on. They said it was an artists' conference and asked if I wanted to register, so I gave the fifteen bucks (because the banquet included all the booze you could drink) and went into this conference room where Catherine was standing up front talking about light and surfaces and how she sculpted using light the way a painter does.

When she finished talking, I went up to her and whispered, "You seem like a nice woman."

She looked surprised, stared at me with evergreen eyes. She laughed. You know, the expected thing was "I enjoyed your talk" or "I admire your work." (I didn't know her work then.)

When she got her words, she said, "You haven't met my husband."

She took my arm and, moving away from the others who'd come to meet her or "fan" her, conducted me to the back of the room, where Ernest was standing against the wall, his arms folded, a sparkle in his eyes.

When we came nearer, he gave me an eagle stare and Catherine a protective one. Catherine introduced us. He shook my hand.

"Can we bring her home with us?" she asked.

"If you want to, Babe," he said.

We laughed like we'd known each other for decades, and I rode squeezed in the back of their Peugeot.

"You're not married?"

"No, I'm a divorcee."

"Goody."

"Why, goody?"

"That means you'll have all the time in the world for us!"

15

"Do you smoke?" Catherine asks.

"No."

"I don't mean tobacco," she says, an imp's grin.

"Not that either."

"What do you like to do? I bet you like to make love," Catherine says. "Look at the girl blush! I've got her tagged there!"

"Catherine's a joker," says Ernest, taking my coat, and going into the kitchen to get the drinks.

"So what do you think of Detroit?" he asks, after we've settled down on the turquoise leather sofa.

(Before yellow, Catherine's color was turquoise.)

Catherine sits on a brown hassock in the middle of the floor, hands on her knees, watching me like I was a movie.

"It's nice, what I've seen of it. I haven't seen much of it. When I got here, I was sort of late, so they spirited me over to the campus, Wayne State University. I haven't seen much."

"Well, when you've seen more of it, I'd like to know what you think of . . ."

"What?"

Ernest sips his Chablis.

"He was going to say 'the murder capital,'" Catherine says.

"What?"

"Private joke," Catherine explains.

"Okay."

"We'll take care of you while you're here," Catherine says

brightly. "You can stay with us. Move out of that wretched hotel."

"I hadn't intended to stay but a couple of days."

"We'd like you to stay with us, wouldn't we, Ernie?"

"Sure."

So I was curious. So I stayed. So I ended up staying several months with them.

At first Catherine tried to fix me up with this part-Black, part-Japanese artist she knew named Koshoo Jackson. He made these beautiful braided belts. I still have the one he gave me but didn't take him up on any other offers. I'll tell you about Koshoo one of these days when I'm in the mood.

"He made these colored braids for me to use on *The Bird-catcher*. He's so beautiful. Why did you cold-shoulder him?"

I sat in a shadowy corner of her studio while she arranged the braids on her sculpture-in-perpetual-progress.

"You're a beast," she said. "Someone to love's not so bad."

I said nothing.

"My two best friends oughta get together."

I raised my eyebrows. Premature declarations of friendship always startled me. I watched her sulk.

Now the braids decorated her waist. Then she had the best idea. She came over and put them in my hair.

"You look sweet. You look just like an Egyptian. Keep 'em."

I gave 'em back.

She dangled them in her arms and pouted, then she draped them around her neck and smiled.

"You might have been such lovers," she said. "I should've planted him in a nightclub, taken you there, and let you pick the beauty for yourself."

16

I'm the woman with crocodile shoulders, telling Catherine weird bitch's story. Who knows what a weird bitch will do? I'll tell you one thing: I'm glad it's not me she's after. This is the paradox: How can a woman claim she loves a man and yet try to be the source of his destruction? And why doesn't the man just get the fuck out? If you ask him he'll give you a bullshit answer like, "She's the most fascinating woman in the world." All the fascinating women in the world could fill the ocean. And as far as I've been able to see it takes one fascinating woman and one ticket to ride the train.

17

Catherine wants to go for a walk on the beach, but no one will go with her. She goes alone and comes back filthy with Ibiza sand, her hair wet, tangled, and matted with seaweed and brine.

"The sea witch," Ernest says.

"You look fucked," I say.

"What were you doing, dragging the fucking ocean?" he asked.

"Thanks," Catherine says. "Fuck the two of you too." She starts out, then turns back. "I almost got myself drowned, you bastards. That young man standing downstairs fished me out."

Ernest and I rush to her. She backs away from us.

"Is the young man still down there?" Ernest asks, fishing into his pockets for coins. "I want to thank him."

"He won't take your fucking money," she says. "What you can do is go wave to him. Let him know I'm okay."

"*Are* you okay?"

She nods.

Ernest goes out on the terrace. We hear his thank-yous, the boy's de nadas. He comes back inside.

"By the way," Catherine asks, "how much would I have been worth?"

She struts out, green weed swaying from the back of her wet head.

"You two should have been with me," she calls. "You two fucking bastards."

18

Ernest tells me about this woman he's writing about in this article on psychokinesis. This woman, he says, redirected her frustrations into psychokinetic energies. She could cause things to move, but she could only cause things to move when she was in a room with her husband. She and her husband would be sitting watching TV and suddenly a lamp would fall and break, or the telephone would start to ring and there'd be no one on the other end, or a chair would slide across the floor or spring into the air. Sometimes there would be more destructive things, like windows breaking, or heavy furniture slamming into walls and doors. At first the couple hired ghost breakers and then discovered through a psychic medium that it was the woman herself causing the destructions and it was her only way of expressing her little dissatisfactions. She hadn't even known she had them. As far as her conscious mind was concerned, theirs was a strong and loving relationship. She loved her marriage and her man.

"Is that how you explain Catherine?"

"I've stopped trying to explain Catherine."

"Why don't you get the fuck out?"

But he doesn't come back with the answer I expect.

"Why don't *you*?"

What can I do but give the bullshit? Not all tickets are made out of paper.

19

Did I tell you about the time we went to this medium? This woman held Catherine's hand and said, "You have a strong love line. Ah, you have a wonderful love line!"

Catherine sniggered because she knew what she was capable of and the woman didn't.

The woman just sat there holding Catherine's hand like she thought the love line would rub off on her.

But then her look changed, and she pushed Catherine's hand out of hers. She pressed her palm to the top of her head and ran.

"And you thought she was a faker," Catherine said. "Nobody can be a faker and fly like that."

20

"Why won't you spend the night with me? It's been so long since we've made love in the dark. Stay with me. I want to hold you in the dark again."

She does not mean for me to hear, but I have come around the corner and into the narrow hallway where they are standing against opposite walls. I back out.

"Come on, you were going to the bathroom, weren't you?" snaps Ernest.

I walk in the tender space between them.

21

It's Catherine's birthday, and there's a birthday cake on the table.

"Go on and cut the cake," Ernest says. "Do you want me to cut it?"

"No." She plunges the plastic knife in and gives Ernest the biggest piece.

"The biggest piece to the greatest love."

There are strawberries and pineapples on top.

"I'd give up everything in a minute if Ernest wanted me to," she says.

"Give what up?" he asks.

"You know what. My work, my sculpture, or anything else."

"I've never asked you to give anything up for me. That's silly," he says, eating his cake. "Why would I ask you to give anything up?"

"Oh, that was the wrong thing to say. Oh, that was wrong!" Catherine storms out.

Ernest, bewildered, cake falling from his mouth, turns to me. "What's this foolishness now? Now what?"

"I'll go see," I say.

Catherine is standing in the hall in front of the bathroom door with blood on her hands.

Perhaps I've been wrong. Perhaps she can be self-destructive too.

"Catherine!"

"It's only my period started. I don't even know what these fucking people call sanitary napkins. What's their word for a sanitary napkin?"

I take off my half-slip, tear it for her, make a pad for her to use.

"We'll walk down the hill and find out what the hell they do call them," I say.

Catherine holds her hands under the faucet and lets cold water run on them.

"Betcha thought I'd pulled a Gwendola, didn't ya?"

I say nothing. I study the water.

"Suppose I did? Do you think he'd forget I'm here?"

I don't answer.

"Do you think it's more moral to pull a Gwendola or a Gauguin?"

"Is she all right?" Ernest calls from outside the door.

"Don't tell him," Catherine whispers.

"She's fine," I say.

"Just the birthday girl blues," sings Catherine. "I'm forty today."

There is a sigh outside the door. I'm not sure whether Catherine hears it through her laughter. I'm sure she doesn't hear my answers to her questions.

22

At breakfast the next day, Catherine won't talk to us. She stares into her plate. She looks betrayed. She slouches.

"Sit up straight," Ernest scolds her. "You don't have to act such a fool because you've turned forty."

"I'm not acting this way because I've turned forty," she pouts.

He tells her he doesn't like self-pity. He tells her to stop pitying herself. She's on this beautiful island and she should be happy. Nothing's wrong with her. There's nothing to pity.

He mentions the faces we saw on TV the other night. Drought and famine victims. They trivialized any of Catherine's complaints, any of ours.

"Can we adopt one of those children?" Catherine had asked. (She said adopt like "adapt.")

"You can't take care of yourself," said Ernest, watching the screen.

"But we ought to be able to save at least one of them. We can ask that friend of yours in Doctors Without Borders. He should know how."

"You can't save yourself," said Ernest.

"He looks like Haile Selassie, doesn't he? Look at that face. You can ask that friend of yours. We should try to save that child."

"You're enough of a child to save."

When they gave the place to send money, Catherine got her checkbook. I couldn't help but think of that Godard movie where

Jack Palance plays the movie producer—"Every time he hears the word 'culture,' he gets out his checkbook." But of course that had nothing to do with this.

And it wasn't the time or place for a joke, not even a dry one.

"Get out your checkbook, Honey," said Catherine.

He got his out.

She glanced at me.

I got out my traveler's checks.

"Forty's good."

"It's not because I'm forty," she says.

"Sit up straight and eat your breakfast. Smile."

She sits up straight, but she doesn't smile. "Can't I be depressed too?" she asks. "Can't I be depressed sometimes like any other woman?"

"If you had something to be depressed about. But you don't. You've got everything."

"Amanda's not sitting up straight. You didn't tell her to sit up straight."

"Listen to this brat. Forty yesterday. Amanda's not *mine*."

"And I *am*."

He's silent, then, "Of course you are."

"Who does Amanda belong to?" she asks, the imp.

He says nothing, then he says, "Well, herself, I suppose, since she's divorced."

"If Amanda's her own, I want to be my own too!"

"Do you want a divorce?"

Catherine stares into her plate, then up. "No chance, buddy. Why should I care if I'm yours or not? *The Birdcatcher*'s mine."

Ernest looks impatient, butters bread.

I stir hard, scrambled eggs. Mushrooms, cheese, green peppers.

"Tell Amanda about when you were a boy and used to hunt foxes," says Catherine, scratching the inside of a nostril.

"Amanda doesn't want to hear about when I used to hunt foxes," says Ernest, impatient, glum.

"To look at this mature, worldly, urbanized intelligent gentle-man you wouldn't believe that he was a rural farm boy from . . ."

"Minnesota," Ernest puts in between bites of buttered toast.

"I didn't know Minnesota grew Black boys, did you?" Cather-ine acts up. "Tell her about when you used to hunt foxes. Tell her about how you catch a fox. This is neat. There's a strategy to it."

Ernest parades the story in monotone. "You catch a fox by sneaking up behind it and grabbing it high up on the tail. You have to grab it high up on the tail, because that locks the spine and it can't spring around and bite you. The first fox I ever tried to catch I didn't grab it far enough up on the tail and it sprang around and bit me."

Catherine raises up his shirt sleeve and shows me the fox bite —a nasty, ragged bite near the tender skin inside his elbow.

"Useful bit of knowledge, isn't it?" Ernest says sourly.

"That's how you catch a woman too," says Catherine, looking into her empty plate like she's trying to read it. "Grab her high enough up on the tail so she won't swing around and bite you."

"That's a more useful piece of knowledge," says Ernest, brightening. "So how does a woman catch a man?"

"She doesn't," says Catherine.

"I thought it was always the woman catching the man," he says.

"That's a myth; it's not true, a woman never catches a man. Never can," she says.

"An old wives' tale?" asks Ernest, and winks at me.

I brighten under his gaze, then glance away, look at Cather-ine, who has spit on her finger and is gathering the last flakes of dried scrambled egg into her mouth—the same finger that had scratched inside her nose.

"Anyway, a woman could never possibly grab a man high enough upon the tail," says Catherine.

"It depends on the woman," says Ernest.

"Aren't we forgetting?" I put in. "Human beings don't have tails."

"Speak for yourself," mumbles Catherine.

"Does that mean we always bite each other?" Ernest asks, the sour look again.

I stare into a stream of sunlight hitting the table, dust particles jostling each other.

"I saw a picture of a human being that had a tail once. In the *Police Gazette*," says Catherine, reading her plate again.

"She means *ordinary* human beings, like us," says Ernest. "We always succeed in biting each other."

"Why don't you just show her? You're clamoring to," blurts Catherine, her tongue like a sliver of pink moon.

Ernest raises up the other sleeve. This time the bite is human. More vicious—deeper, wider, darker. Catherine looks at it like one might look at a trophy.

"That impossible woman," she whispers. Then louder, "I've got to go pee. Let me up."

Rebuttoning his sleeve, Ernest stands. Catherine slides out of the booth and heads toward the toilet. I go with her. That's the policy. Once when they were in some public place, Catherine had gone to the bathroom, discovered this sliver that had broken off the top of the commode, hid it like a dagger in her coat. Well, you know the rest.

I stand inside the door puffing on a cigarette.

"You know what this is like," Catherine says, her pee sounding like a faucet gushing.

"What?"

"Well, you get here and let me stand up there all self-contained and that La Gioconda smile and you'd know what the fuck it was like."

"Stop talking dirty."

"Words to live by," she says. The pee trickles, then stops. She's one of those who wipe from behind. She farts.

There's the clearing of a throat in the booth next door.

"Howdy, neighbor," shouts Catherine. Her teeth flash Bugs Bunny and she knocks on the wall.

The woman flushes. There's a hurried assembling of garments.

"Surf's up," calls Catherine.

As there's the sound of the woman's door opening, Catherine pushes me aside, pikes her head out the door, and shouts, "Here's Johnny!"

The startled woman flees.

"She probably thinks we're crazy," says Catherine, pulling up her drawers.

23

On the island of Ibiza, I see two old women whipping each other with tree branches. I ask them, "Why are you whipping each other?"

They answer, "For errors we made when we were young women like you."

When Catherine and I are two old women, will we take up branches, too, whip each other, and complain of errors we've made?

I hope not. I hope we'll hug each other instead.

In the meantime, I turn from the "donkey path" and hunt a beach.

24

Catherine sits with a yellow towel under her; I sit on a blue one. We absorb the sun. I rub coconut oil onto my knees and shoulders, and into the flakes of crocodile skin.

"I want a daughter," Catherine says.

I think of the TV faces.

"Why don't you have a daughter for me? You and Ernest? I'd love her like my own. She *would* be my own. She'd be *our* own."

She touches my stomach lightly.

"We'd love her so much!"

"I'm too old," I say. I cannot bring myself to tell her the truth of it.

"Women have children into their forties," says Catherine. "I know a woman who had a child at fifty-five. Some places in Russia . . ."

"Why don't you have your own daughter?

"He wanted to in the beginning when we were first married, but I wanted to put it off, because of my work, and then when I was ready I couldn't."

"That's a pity," I say.

"So you see you have to do this. We'll bring her up in our postcard places." He'd told her. When? Making love?

"No, Catherine."

Catherine sits, biting her bottom lip. Then she reaches into her purşe and takes one of the melt-in-your-mouth sedatives the doctors have given her. Then she looks at me out of hooded eyes.

Finally, she rises and walks along the beach looking for scavenger objects to use in her sculptures. In her early sculptures she used wrenches, screwdrivers, radio parts, plumber's tools, but now she is not allowed such things and must seek safer objects. She collects them in the towel: shells, dried starfish, the top of an abandoned bikini bathing suit.

Ernest or I will check her before she enters with them. We constantly check her studio and other hiding places in the house. It's agreed upon, terms of her release. It's expected.

Anyone watching would not know that they're watching a dangerous woman. Anyone watching would think Catherine's perfectly harmless and perfectly beautiful. You've seen them—those endearing strangers—Oh, I bet she'd be just wonderful to know!

I watch her reach down and scoop up shadows. I'll check on her return to find out whether any of the shadows are dangerous.

"I underwent hypnosis when I had her," says Gillette, showing us a picture of herself holding a bald-headed baby Tatum, Tatum blonde and white as starch and bewildered. "I was afraid. I was unspeakably afraid. The doctors thought my psychological state would harm both of us, because they said they'd never seen a woman as afraid as I was. So they put me under hypnosis, so that I could feel in control of my baby. Uh, my body, I mean."

She lights a cigarette, scratches the inside of her thighs, where a rash or heat bumps can be seen. We're sitting in the trailer, at the kitchen table, drinking coffee, and Tatum is somewhere in the front playing. "This is killing me. Some allergy. The doctors don't know what the fuck it is.

"I had a twenty-four-hour labor. Can you imagine what it would have been like if I hadn't gone under? They used to think hypnosis was magic, but it's not. All those Svengali movies. At first, I used to think they were all fakers, and then when I believed in them, I didn't think they could put me under hypnosis, not this girl. I thought if you had a strong mind, then it wouldn't work.

But they say it doesn't matter how strong your mind is. And it's very logical, very scientific, but still you have to trust the person hypnotizing you. I don't know what I would have done otherwise. But hypnosis made it beautiful. The hypnosis made it like opening a door. I was proud afterwards, of myself. And they say that after I had her I was just smiling. That I was looking the way that every woman should look. As soon as she was out, and they pulled her up where I could see her, just this great smile. 'That's the way every woman should look,' I heard one of the nurses say. I wish I could have seen myself. I bet it wasn't just those little Gioconda smiles either. They couldn't paint the way I must have looked. I guess I didn't want to have to *work* to have her. I know this sounds awful. I didn't want to have to *work* to have her. I wanted her, but without the *work*, without that kind of work, you know. Cathy, you should have a child."

Catherine sits with her mouth slightly open. She says nothing.

"I don't suppose you want one, though, do you?" asks Gillette.

"It's too complicated," Catherine says.

"Oh, yes, I wish it could be simple and easy. Some women, though, make it look simple and easy. They say that acupuncture can relieve the pain too. I don't believe in drugs. But Cathy, if there hadn't been hypnosis, I don't know what I would have done. But Amanda's a joy."

"Amanda?"

"That's Tatum's name, her real name." She glances at me. "She just wants me to call her Tatum, you know. But her name's Amanda, because she's worth being loved. Her nickname's Sister. But she wants me to call her Tatum, like the little girl in the movies." She calls out. "Come here, darling. Where's my darling?"

Tatum comes running and climbs into her lap.

"What have you been doing, playing in the mud? You're so untidy, you're a little root hog." She kisses Tatum on the jaw, making blubbery noises. "You're my angel, though, aren't you, baby? You're my little sweet angel."

Book 11   *Who Was the*
           Last One to
           Call You Darling?

25

I can't remember exactly what the name of the disease was, but I think he called it hairy nevus or hairy nervous. *Ebony* printed this article once about a woman whose skin started turning white in patches until she was all white. I like to clip such articles. I used to like to clip those weird stories from the *Police Gazette*. Catherine and I felt we'd been fated to meet since we'd both been childhood fans of that magazine. Perhaps it's turned into the *National Inquirer*. The *Police Gazette*'s strange tales, though, always seemed more well-bred.

Anyway, instead of turning all white, this Brazilian only turned white from the waist down, as if the disease were equipped with some kind of reasoning or radar and knew exactly where it wanted to go. There was even a fine line like an equator around his waist.

"Most women are surprised or frightened," he says, after he has taken his trousers off, and I see his white legs and feet and his equator belly. "But you, you must have seen something like this before, or heard of it?"

"No, you're the first."

"And you're not afraid of me? Every other woman has been. One woman took one look at me and ran."

I stay put. He takes his drawers off. He touches my breasts with his black hands. I stare at his white feet. Finally, I stare at his privates. He kisses my nipples. He cannot believe I am neither

73

surprised nor afraid of him. "Surprise and fear are the same," he says. He opens my legs and enters me.

"I can't believe this," he says.

"Believe it."

He kisses my mouth; he nibbles my tongue and lips. When he gets to the crocodile skin on my back, he touches it as if it were familiar territory.

"You're a tender, mysterious woman and I'm an alien in my own country. We belong to each other."

Catherine would love that love talk. In Portuguese it sounds lovely. In English it sounds like bullshit. Take your pick.

But I can't tell Catherine about him, though, because one day I'd discover him staring down at me from some museum. This strange man. All black above the navel, all white below it, and people wondering what was the symbolism, what was the metaphor. And some woman saying, "Why, it's the country, my dear." And another: "Well, shouldn't he be white above and black below?"

I did get him to be braver, though, to go for a walk with me on the beach and even wear his bathing trunks.

"They don't know what manner of man I am," he whispers. "Or what kind of woman you are to be with such a man!"

26

The walls of the room look like they've been polished with talc and oil. Lace curtains hang at the windows—pattern of two birds of paradise facing each other. Kissing? Shades lowered. Lemony smell. You'd swear it came from the carpet—thick and yellow. Catherine would love them. Gilded mirror. Ensinanco made it himself when he worked one summer in a mirror factory. A bench-like love seat, the dresser, the bed, the mirror, carpets, and that's all. Paradise.

27

"Come here, Amanda," Catherine says. "I want you to speak to someone."

She's holding the phone out to me, the cord wrapped around her wrist, so that she has to unwrap it before I can take it.

"Who is it?" I whisper. Behind her the sun is orange.

"Someone for *you*."

I pick it up and he says, "Darling, is that you? How are you?"

As if I'd never left, as if I were only in the apartment next door, visiting neighbors, as if I'd never left.

I slam the phone down, while Catherine's standing there smiling.

"Don't do that again."

"I thought you'd be happy. I thought hearing his voice would make you happy." She's perched against the back of the couch, her arms folded.

"Don't meddle in things you don't know anything about. I put up with Koshoo but not this."

"Then tell me about him."

"It's all my business, you hear. How did you learn his name anyway?"

"You're the little fool," she says. "Who else but a little fool would be divorced and go around with their fucking luggage tag still saying 'Mrs. Lantis Wordlaw,' and giving the old fucking address and telephone number?"

I say nothing. I would go now and tear the tags off and replace them with new ones. But I'm too lazy and I don't want to see her gloat more than she's doing now. So I merely stand there and watch Catherine, whose mouth is shaped like a Cheerio.

"Lantis, that's an unusual name," she observes.

"It's short for Atlantis. His parents named him Atlantis, but the children teased and kidded him too much. Lantis was easier. When he grew up, he had it legally changed."

"I like Atlantis better."

"So do I. So does he now that he's older and knows better."

"Will he change it back?"

I shrug.

She still has the Cheerio mouth.

"I bet you're not divorced. Legally," she says. "I bet you just ran away from him."

I say nothing.

"I like that," she says pensively. "The idea of the woman doing the running, the abandoning."

"I didn't abandon."

"Did you tell him first or did you just disappear?"

"I just disappeared."

"Go get 'em, tiger!" she yells, clapping hands, and prancing about the room. "I know!"

But she does not know. She does not know about the girl. She does not know that I put the phone down so quickly because in the next instance he'd have put Panda on the line. And that would have been too hard. That would have been the hard thing. That would have been the thing to turn this witch into glass.

"I know!" Jumping up, she's an ostrich dancing. Old-fashioned silk blouse with ruffles in the back. She dips her arms, then springs up. "I know!"

She does not know how straight my face gets when I lie.

28

"I think it's a rotten idea," Ernest says.

"What?" I ask, sitting down to breakfast and shaking salt into a cantaloupe half.

We're on the terrace. She's painted the chairs and table yellow. The sun's yellow.

"I told Ernest about our idea."

"What idea?"

"I don't think it was Amanda's idea," says Ernest. "I don't think she'd have anything to do with such a silly idea."

"What idea?"

"She doesn't even remember," sulks Catherine. Her famous betrayed look. She stands up to leave the table.

"Sit down and eat your breakfast," says Ernest.

She sits back down.

"What idea?" I persist.

"The baby!"

"That wasn't *my* idea."

She glares at me. "I'd never leave a man who was in love with me."

"I'd never try to kill one," I want to blurt, but instead I say, "Forget it."

I plunge my spoon into the cantaloupe. When I stare into Catherine's eyes again, she's scratching inside her nostril, looking as if she's already forgotten. Ernest reaches over and dabs cantaloupe juice from her jaw, plucks her finger from her nose like she's the wayward brat herself.

Catherine shrinks down in her chair. Now she's the shrinking woman.

"How are you?" he asks.

"Okay," she says, and shrinks down further.

A woman stands in the window of a building across the street, shaking out a quilt. She eyes us, then she retreats into the recesses of shadow. I wonder if she's still watching.

"I won't be spending the day with you two girls," he says. "*Psychology Today* is waiting for that article I was telling you about and I've got to finish it today."

"You can't leave! Spend at least part of the day with us. Let's go cycling."

"I can't, Catherine. Work to do."

"Take a hike then." She thumbs her nose.

In spite of her, he stands and kisses her and waves to me. Catherine won't look at him. She shrinks down further.

"Why do you have to be such a fucking bore? You're such a fucking bore. What a bore. You're both two fucking bores."

He stands watching her a moment, then he leaves. Suddenly, she springs up, a full-blown woman again. I watch him entering the streets below. He waves to us from the street, without turning around.

"We three used to have such *fun*," Catherine says. "Do you remember what a good time we used to have? How we used to *play*? You're both such bores now."

"You can't play all the time."

"Well at least he can keep Saturdays for play."

Down below, a man in a straw hat leads a donkey whose back is loaded with straw chairs tied with a rope. The man spends his days weaving straw chairs. I wonder what such a life is like.

"Bores."

"You used to say that just being in our company made you happy. Now we have to perform for you."

"Why not? Like the song says, 'Everybody wants to be in show business.'"

"Is that what you're in?"

"Say what?"

"Show business. Or what my folks call 'showing off.' Is that what you're doing? 'Showing off' every time you try it? Are you so fucking bored that trying to kill him adds the only excitement . . . ?"

"Anyway, is that why you left your husband?" she asks.

"What?"

"Because he was a fucking bore? Because you were so fucking bored?"

I won't give her that. I won't agree to it.

"People bore themselves."

"Bullshit. I never bore myself."

She shrinks down in her chair again.

"Did he ever make you feel *small*? That's what I really mean." She needed to know.

"Yeah," I give her. "I guess so. I guess at times. All men do at times. So they can feel men I guess."

"He makes me feel small all the time. Small all the time."

She's already a small woman, and right now there's peach fuzz in the corner of her mouth. Electrolysis, baby.

"Small's not paradise."

Yeah, I could be telling her, I've known men like that, who make me feel smaller than I suspect I am. But when I think of Ernest, I think of the opposite. I feel full-blown or larger than I suspect I am. A better woman. But I cannot tell her that. But don't we all want to be in the presence of someone who makes us feel larger and better than what we can ourselves imagine we could ever be?

"I feel like he's standing on my head," says Catherine. "I feel like he's standing on my head and hammering me down."

It is unfair of me to tell her what I can or can't believe of the man. Certainly I cannot see the Ernest that she sees, but then she can't see—all right I'll say it—*my* Ernest.

My Ernest? Describe to you the Ernest I see? Married to an impossible woman. Bewildered and bemused by his situation. He wants to see his wife happy and productive, and he tries to put her in places that will allow her to be. There are his types, I suppose; you know them: big, protective, nurturing men, the ones you think about when you're in trouble (and out of it) but who seem always there for the rescue of others (and you wonder who rescues them); two-hearted men, I call them, like Hemingway described that river. Sometimes I imagine I'm here for his rescue as much as Catherine's; at least I fly to them as much for his sake as hers, to steer him as much as I can out of harm's way.

Or that time Catherine dragged me to this crystal museum— they had these giant crystals from every part of the world, and every color—and you walked around them and at every angle it was like discovering some wonder, the way the light showed in and around and jumped out of them. I liked the way Catherine described it: "They've got goodies any which way you look!" How do I remember him in those early days? How did we chat?

I remember once I flew to them:

"Here you are," he said.

We sat on the steps outside the psychiatric hospital together. Just sat. Occasionally, he would just glance over at me, regarding me, but I wouldn't look back at him. I no longer asked him why. I'd stopped asking him why first. Anybody's guess, and anybody's guess was as good as the next fellow's. I could feel his eyes on me. I started thinking of something else I read once in a book by Hemingway, his island book. That painting was practiced by better people than writing. She was a sculptor though. Same difference. She'd tried to kill him, and yet somehow the idea of Catherine as "the better person" always ran through my head. Because of that book? Well, who are you in the next guy's imagination? Is it hard to be the person in your own?

"They're putting her on a different sort of medication," he said. "She has to take it for ten years. My God, and what happens afterwards? I don't know what they mean."

Something else he (the other Ernest, Hemingway) said. That if he were a good enough person he'd have been a painter, that if one were enough of a bastard, he'd be a good writer. Something like that. I must have read it years ago but only remembered it when I met Catherine and became part of her troupe.

Creature of her own invention. When you say that again, Cowgirl, smile.

Why does he stay with her?

Can you be better than your actions?

If I were bastard enough I'd . . .

He kept turning to look at me, but I wouldn't look back.

"Do you know how well I think of you?" he asked.

"For coming?"

"Not just for coming, but for coming too . . . I'm not handling it very well."

"Better than most."

"I spoke with her doctor, but they never tell you anything you can use."

"So should I come back tomorrow?"

"Yeah, it's better to wait. Tomorrow's soon enough."

His gray suit wrinkled in spots and places.

"I can come and pick you up tomorrow if you want."

"No, that's too much trouble, and besides your hotel's closer. I'm out of your way."

He was silent, observing me.

"There's almost nothing I wouldn't do for you; you know that," he said.

I heard the "almost." Does every woman hear the "almost"?

"Thanks, but I can get here."

"Okay."

"Your suit looks like it's been through somebody's mill."

That was the polite cliche. I mean I could have slipped and told him he looked like something the Cat dragged in.

And Catherine—she wouldn't like this description—she's one of those people who can always succeed at making an entrance—a grand entrance (though her entrances are mostly private ones, into living rooms and onto terraces where Ernest and I are seated). But I've seen her enter public places too, restaurants, museums, stores. To tell the truth, she's not a particularly attractive woman; still she's one of those women that people look at and say "What a beauty!" That's a paradox Ellison would like too, a riddle for Joyce. When she enters a room you look up. You don't go back to what you were doing; you keep looking. You look till she's settled somewhere and then occasionally you'll glance back. You don't particularly notice the people with her, just figure they must be special too to be with such a woman. If you don't know her, the first thing you'll wonder is if she's one of those theatrical people, one who's just come from a performance. Like when she first straightened her hair again after ten years, she came in with this pageboy (she insists it's an Egyptian cut), straight bangs across the front, and back, and hanging diamond earrings. (She calls me "the last stubborn woman" because I've kept my afro.) Well, anyway, she comes in with her newly straightened hair and her face looking like fresh paint and declares, "Take me out to dinner, y'all!" Well, I will admit, I did think of Cleopatra, but it's the meaning of Nefertiti's name that popped in my head—"The beautiful woman has come!"

Well, we take her out to dinner and the people's heads pop up, and they keep staring until we've been shown to a table. If people looked at me that way, I'd think it was because I had spinach stuck in my teeth or a dangling booger. But Catherine seems oblivious to it—she's wearing these spiked heels, a yellow dress, and a turquoise shawl draped regally on her shoulders, and looking very *French* (Martinican she'll insist). So after we've settled and made ourselves comfortable the people go back to their din-

ner but occasionally I'll see them look up—eyes go straight for
Catherine—like it matters if she's eating or smiling, bewildered
or amused, reading her plate, or scratching her little brown nose.

Once we saw people like that ourselves. We were sitting in
a restaurant in New York and this woman came in, a "theatrical person" who out-Catherined Catherine. She was in a crowd
with these other people wearing this purple dress and a long purple scarf. She was in a crowd with these others, but your eyes
zoomed right to her and stayed there. Even Catherine was staring. The woman was taller than Catherine, darker, with a forest
crop of hair. She had the sort of eyes you don't forget. "Endur-
ing," I heard someone call them once. It's funny. Catherine and I
looked at her, but Ernest just ate his food. I wondered at the time
whether women other women find interesting are ever found interesting by men. Or maybe he was just being discreet. Anyway,
Catherine and I kept our attention on her and her crowd. She
kept wrapping and unwrapping her scarf; I remember that, and
something she said made me think she and I had gone to the same
school: "That sounds exactly like Sojourner Truth. You all know
who Sojourner Truth was, don't you?"

"Eat," Ernest said, slightly nudging Catherine.

Catherine glanced up at me. "I bet they're theater people,"
she murmured.

"Yeah, they could be," I said.

"What theater people?" asked Ernest, spearing one of his
steamed potatoes.

"Maybe we can take in a show," said Catherine. "You know,
we have been to New York three times straight in as many years
and have not seen one show. It seems a sin to come to New York
and not see a show, even if Ernest does think they all stink."

"I never said they all stink."

"You said Broadway stinks."

"I don't remember saying Broadway stunk." He glanced over
at the "theater" crowd for a minute but didn't seem to take any

special notice. He glanced at me, then Catherine. "Maybe it was the season."

"I don't think you understand the theater." To me. "He likes everybody's music in the world; it's all good music to him, but he doesn't understand the theater."

"Because I don't like everything?"

"I think it's a sin to come to New York and not go to a show."

"I'll remember that," I said with a laugh.

"I hope I don't see my line in one of your books," said Catherine, pouting. "You're a regular snapping turtle; you snap up everything. Ernest saw one of his lines in your last book."

"What line?"

"I don't remember which one, do you Ern?"

"Hmm." He was chewing. He swallowed. "I don't remember. Something about decadence, I think."

"It had to do with decadence, I know that. Well, anyway, he saw his line, and he was really pleased and flattered. I'm telling you right now I wouldn't be flattered at all. Anyway, I'm going to make myself a little fortune-cookie-like strip of paper and paste that line to one of my own works. It's mine, do you hear?"

She tapped my knuckles with her fork. A piece of melted cheese stuck to a knuckle. I licked it off. I thought of Fitzgerald forbidding Zelda to use certain experiences. This one's mine; you can have that one. Oh, but you took the best experience!

The woman with the scarf said something. It was loud enough to get the voice but not the words.

"She has a voice like a warning, doesn't she?" Ernest asked.

Catherine glanced at me and waved her little finger, then she scratched her nose. "You can have that one. I'm generous tonight."

"Maybe we can try Off-Broadway," said Ernest.

"Now do yourself," Catherine would say if she read to this point. But I can't do myself. You can never do yourself. Even with my descriptions of Catherine and Ernest, and the little scenes, every other person in the world would come along and describe them differently. Are those the folks? Not only are we ourselves as different from others as snowflakes, but we're as different from ourselves as snowflakes in the way that others would describe us, and sometimes even in the many ways that we'd describe ourselves. Have a thousand people describe Catherine and you'll have a thousand Catherines. Have a thousand people sit on those steps with Ernest, or at that table in New York, and you'd have a thousand scenes. Like that time Catherine was reading the international issue of *Time* and started laughing. "What?" I asked.

"This story," she said. "Every time I read it, it's different. To one person it's a heroic act, to another it's villainous, to yet another it's just foolishness. Why don't you write a novel like that?"

"I already have," I said.

"You have?"

"You know the one called *Joker*. Seen from three different perspectives—these three people tell the story of the same event, and when you get through reading it you hold the three views simultaneously or you don't know which to hold: the person's a hero, a villain, or a joke."

"But you must think joke?"

"Why?"

"Because you name it *Joker*."

"No, I don't think joke; I think hero. I name it *Joker* because . . ."

"You're the joker," she said. "It's the author who's the joker!"

"Darn right," I said, lifting an imaginary hat to her, and stirring the lemon in my martini.

29

Speaking of jokers, speaking of the ways we hold different views of people, here's my meeting with Koshoo Jackson I never gave the full account of. (Those of you who know Japanese will also get the joke inside the joke.) Anyway, here's the scene or the scenario:

When Catherine went into the kitchen, Koshoo asked, "Do you feel it too?"

"Yes," I said.

"Mother Eagle hovering, ready to feed us . . ."

"Each other?" I asked.

"You're a woman after my own heart."

He took something out of his pocket, placed it across my knees. At first I thought it was one of those fake snakes you get from joke and curio shops. But it was so slender, beautiful, and delicate. A lavender braid.

"Oh, this is marvelous," I said, fingering it.

"In Japan making braids is a very ancient and respected art form."

I'd seen them decorating kimonos and statues. I nodded. But I really hadn't thought of it as an art form in itself, as a self-contained art.

"When I first started doing it here they treated me like some wayward fellow making doilies."

"It's really very beautiful."

"It's for you."

"I really can't take it," I said.

I couldn't take it from a fellow I'd cold-shouldered all evening, and after this island of congeniality, intended to cold-shoulder the rest of the time.

The smell of beef and okra drifted from the kitchen. I tried to identify the spices: pepper, sage, garlic, paprika. You can't smell salt, can you?

"What's she making?"

"I don't know. Something she got from the Islands."

"It smells like the Islands."

"Did you notice how they both managed to disappear at just the right moment? This has been orchestrated," he said, raising his eyebrows.

He had very black hair, straight in parts, nappy in others. Nappy along the edges. He wore a braid down his back, a green corduroy jacket and black trousers. He was a very handsome man, looked expensive, looked well taken care of. His father had studied Japanese in college, he said, at a time when it seemed the strangest thing in the world for a Black man to be doing. But when the war came his knowledge of Japanese came in handy, and he was recruited for army intelligence, translating technical reports and trying to break codes. After the war he went to Japan, to see the horrors of the war, and met a young woman there, and fell in love. After he told me that one, he said that he was just an army brat whose father had been stationed in Japan after the war, helping the Japanese rebuild after the destruction. But the love affair was true. His mother was from a family of Japanese artists—braid makers. He grew up in a regular braid-making factory. (I learned later from Catherine—at least her account of him or his account to her—that his father had been a merchant marine. But whatever his father had been, the love part always surfaced.)

"I like you a lot," he said. "Why don't we blow this joint?" He spoke in his best Bogie accent.

"We can't," I said. "We can't spoil Catherine's dinner."

"It isn't working," he said, "because you don't want it to work. I know you like me."

I fingered the braid across my knees. I handed it back to him. He returned it to his jacket pocket. (I got it again later; I'll let you guess how.)

"What's the story?" he asked then.

"No story."

"You've got such beautiful wide eyes." He fingered my eyebrows, fingered the space between my eyes, fingered my chin, moved my face toward his and kissed me.

"I'm going to have a showing in Paris next week. Why don't you come with me?"

"I can't."

"Think about it."

I said nothing. He smelled like a pinecone.

"Anyway, my braids didn't do anything spectacular here in the States until Catherine and I combined our talents—we had a joint showing where she used the braids to decorate her sculptures. It made a sensation and I've been in demand in America and Europe ever since."

"What about Japan?"

"Oh, in Japan I'm just a second-rate braid maker. They wouldn't even look at me in Japan."

"That didn't look second rate to me."

But I remember this Sri Lanka story we'd read in a creative writing class where the teacher insisted on using materials from different cultures, rather than just Western literature, and everyone in the class had marveled at how wonderful and original the story was; how impeccably written, every element so precise and meticulous like a fine oriental tapestry (or a Billie Holiday tune I put in, to the class's dismay); how superb the storyteller's imagination! But the teacher said he'd shown the story to an acquaintance from Sri Lanka and the fellow laughed—said in Sri Lanka that it was the most conventional, mundane, ordinary story that anyone could write. In fact, in Sri Lanka it would have been the work of a third-rate storyteller.

"It's a very ancient art there," he was saying. "My mother's people laughed at me. Her grandfather was celebrated as the best braid maker in Japan. I'm decent, that's all."

I still marveled. But I said nothing. And I didn't want him to give me any more details of himself, his life. (Make believe or real?) I didn't want to be drawn closer. I didn't want to be intrigued by anyone someone else had arranged for me to meet. I liked to collide with a lover by chance. But how could I tell him what the problem was or make sense of it? "If I'd picked you out of a crowd," I could have said. Then he'd say, "Let's go find a crowd."

He held out his palm. I put my hand inside it.

"Have you ever been to Paris?" he asked.

"Passed through."

"How can you pass through Paris? Woman, you're something else!"

He hugged my shoulder, and I leaned into him.

But when Catherine came back and Ernest returned with the wine, I didn't say one word to him. I wouldn't behave naturally, though the three of them joked and reminisced. Occasionally, he'd glance at me, offer a smile that I would not return, until they stopped being offered. At the door, I offered him a hand. Cold fish and chilled Spumante.

"So long."

My look said, "Don't make anything of it."

His: "Not to worry."

Catherine, all gay, colorful, swirling-print dress, walked him to the elevator.

When she came back inside I was in the kitchen stacking dishes.

"You behaved like an ass tonight," she said.

"I ate your Cracker Jacks," I said, "but I'm not eating the prize."

"What the fuck are you talking about? You could have behaved better to our friend."

She turned the kitchen light on. I'd been working by the light from the hallway.

"I don't like to be set up," I said. "I don't like to be fixed up."

"Who fixed you up?" she said. "We're all friends here."

I said nothing.

"Anyway, so what's wrong with being fixed up with a prize like that?" she asked.

I regretted having used the metaphor of prize. Worse than "doll" for a woman.

"I like picking a man out of a crowd, by chance," I explained.

"So let's go find you a crowd. Just give me time to plant Ko-shoo in it."

"Too late now," I said, throwing a glance at her, digging in her nose, oblivious. Then she seemed to snap to attention, in the world again.

"You're a fool," she said. "If I didn't have Ernest I'd grab that doll myself."

I grimaced, started filling the sink with soap and water.

"What are you doing?" she asked.

"Washing dishes."

"What the fuck do you think I've got a fucking dishwasher for?" she asked.

She popped open the door of it and we stacked the dishes inside.

"Just promise you won't try to fix me up again," I said. "I'm perfectly capable."

She snapped the dishwasher door closed and pushed a button.

"All right, kiddo," she said. "But me, if I were free, Black, a woman, and over thirty-five I'd . . ."

"Use the dishwasher?" I asked.

She looked at me. A traffic light turning from red to green.

"You darn right. You darn right. You darn right. My clock's working, babe, even if yours isn't. I know I'm no spring chicken."

She took hold of my elbow and we "no spring chickens" marched into the living room, where Ernest greeted us with a beautiful wide smile.

"Did you see how this woman behaved?" she asked, dropping my elbow and giving me a "naughty girl" look.

"She behaved all right to me," he said. "How was she supposed to behave?"

"When he's eating he wouldn't notice the devil," said Catherine, dropping down on the sofa.

"I'd notice the devil," he said.

"Yeah, if he went after your grits."

"I'd give him my grits; it's my prime rib I'd put up a struggle for," he joked. Then he glanced at me. "You weren't bad, kid. I thought you handled yourself real well."

Catherine sat shaking her head.

"I thought she treated that lovely man unforgivably," she said.

"Ah, Koshoo'll get over it. He thinks he's a lady-killer anyway. I guess he's got enough evidence to back him up." He winked at me. "I'm glad to see there's one lady he didn't kill."

Catherine sulked. Reload the cameras, folks. There's at least three Koshoo Jackson's here.

30

"You dream with your eyes open."

"What?"

"You were dreaming with your eyes open."

"How did you know I was dreaming?"

"Because you were laughing and shaking your woolly head."

I sit up in the peacock chair, and Catherine is standing over me.

"I bet you just scare your lovers."

"What?"

"They wake up in the middle of the night and find you dreaming with your fucking eyes open. I bet you scare them out of their trees."

"Some of them."

"What do they do?"

"The smart ones run."

"What do the others do?"

"What do you think?"

"Fuck the zombi."

31

"It's strange, isn't it?" Encobierta asked.

We were walking in her herb garden. I'd shown her the flakey, scaly skin on my back, and she said she had just the herb, brewed in tea, that would cure it. She was reaching down to tear up the plant now.

"Yes, I don't know, it just suddenly started; my skin started scaling."

"I meant what happened to him. Besides his thing, yours is a little thing; yours is a chigger. I can't cure his by snatching up ipecacuanha. His is heaven's punishment; it can only be cured by heaven."

"Why do you call it heaven's punishment?"

"Because he turned his back on his destiny."

Her back was turned to me as she squatted and pulled up the weed. She was wearing blue jeans and a purple blouse. Her rear end was broad and flat. She had no waist. Her hair was a frizzy gray and tied in a knot in the back. It looked like it had been rubbed with mink oil. She smelled like oranges.

"I won't call him Ensinanco anymore. I won't call him by his real name. I call him Ensinadelo; that means heaven's punishment. But he's changed his own name."

"What was his destiny?"

"To be a *curandero*, a curer."

"Like you?"

"I'm no curer. I fool with herbs, that's all. I'm a little amateur healing woman, but my profession's keeping inns, and keeping travelers happy with clean rooms and good food in the belly. But Ensinadelo was born with the gift. He was born with it. When he was just a baby, a little crawling baby, he touched a man's ailment and healed it.

"But when he got older, he didn't want to have a thing to do with it. He wanted to have something to do with the modern world, he said. He doubted his powers, anyway; he said it wasn't his powers that healed; it was ignorant country folks' superstitions."

She had turned to face me now but was still squatting on the ground, holding a green plant in her fist. The garden wasn't symmetrical like English gardens, but it was allowed to grow wild and haphazard, and one wondered how she found the herbs she'd planted. There were little paths for one to walk, but there was no pattern or logic to them, not even the pattern and logic one finds in a maze. I could see the inn from where we were standing, but I would certainly need her to guide me out.

"Then when he went off to the university, it was to study to be an engineer so he could work in Rio, to be a modern man for modern times. What good is the gift of healing if it can't be used in modern times as well as ancient ones? Look at you, a thoroughly modern Millie, aren't you? And what do American doctors tell you?"

"They don't know what"—(I left off "the fuck")—"I have. One doctor said he thought it was caused by nerves, another by taking too many baths. But if I'd followed the latter's instructions, I'd be a stink bucket."

She laughed, rose up.

"We'll go back up and I'll show you how to brew the tea," she said. "It's all internal. It all starts from the inside. We're going to brew it with cactus water, but any water will do."

I followed her. She was wearing flat, practical shoes, ringed with tan and brown. The muscles in her buttocks rippled as she walked; her shoulders danced.

"He used to be able just to touch someone and cure them,"

she said. "Sometimes he didn't even have to put his mind to it—just touch them—like if you jostled someone in a crowd, if he happened to touch someone who needed some cure they'd be cured. How can he say that's ignorant folks' belief, when they knew nothing to believe!"

He touched my back during our lovemaking I was thinking, and it was still . . .

"But probably now," she was saying, "he couldn't heal a mite. That's what happens to you if you've got a power and you refuse to use it; you lose it."

Was she trying to tell me she knew about . . . ?

"If he turns to it again, maybe he'll get the healing powers back. But they won't come easy like before. They'll come like judgment."

I stood in the kitchen as she plunged the plant into boiling water, lifted it from the stove, and poured me some. Another batch she let sit in the sun to make sun tea. She sipped some herself because she said it was good for other problems, problems of spirit as well as physical ones.

"Me? I'm an amateur healing woman. I have only a joking relationship with it, but him, what a *curandero* he could have been!"

She was silent.

"I also have a plant that has contraceptive powers," she said. "That's why there's only Ensinadelo."

I said nothing.

"In the beginning, you see, I feared him. If one crawling baby had such power! I was a young girl without much understanding. Not ignorant, no, but without much understanding."

I said nothing.

"Do you think you'll have any use for it?"

"Understanding?"

She laughed. "That other plant."

"No," I said, too quickly. I was always shy with older women about such matters, though we all knew where the oysters were, as I heard a fisherman's wife say once; around younger women and my peers I had more bravado.

"Don't I look like a grown woman?" she asked. "Do you think I think it's just a joking relationship?"

I laughed. "Everything's okay. Everything's set," I said, and tried to make a jest of it. "I don't leave home without it," I said, trying to put on my best Karl Malden grin.

She sipped her tea.

"I've had a lot of women stay here," she said, after a moment. "I like you best, but the others, too, as soon as he appears, make cow eyes at him, and he starts throwing sweetheart lances—love lances—at them." She looked at me carefully.

"I know," I said. "I guessed."

"The flirting looks in the beginning," she said. "Then very abruptly, they leave."

I said nothing. I could feel my bowels loosen. I shifted in my chair, stayed seated.

"You've braved it the longest."

"I'm not braving it."

"If he hadn't run off and tried to pursue another destiny that wasn't meant for him—maybe you're just one of the weird ones, or maybe because of your own little malady—but I like you anyway . . . Have they loosened yet?"

"What?"

"Your bowels."

"They're too loose."

"You better run, girl," she sang the American rock song.

I couldn't hold my laugh or my shit in.

When I came back, bathed and changed, she said, "That's only the first clearing out. It won't have that same effect anymore. I mean, you can sip it anyplace, anytime, carry it around in a thermos. I'll dry some for you, so that you can take it with you."

"When I leave?" I asked.

"Don't worry," she said, scratching her neck. "I know you're

not those other women, that you're not leaving because of *him*.
You're leaving because of yourself. You'd leave even if he were
some ordinary stranger."

"Man," I said.

She sucked at her teeth. "Yeah, even if he were just some everyday man."

32

Ensinadelo (Ensinanco) and I pulled the lounge beach chairs into the sun. The air was clear. I wondered if his white legs would sunburn. I rubbed Vaseline and cocoa butter onto them. This was the first time he'd been brave enough to wear swimming trunks. Of course people stared. They gawked. How could you expect them not to? In fact, I could tell nationalities by the way they looked at him. Americans were the first to gawk, to stand and gawk, and no bones about it. One American even took his picture (not up close of course, but from a safe distance), took several pictures, and then came back and took another one. The English looked once and were done with looking. The French looked, were amazed and fascinated, but pretended they weren't looking. The Swedes looked, came over, and jovially discussed the matter with us. The Germans looked, pretended they weren't looking, and pretended furthermore that there was nothing phenomenal in a man made thus, no different from any other ordinary human being; if he had had a belly made out of a tin drum they'd have pretended he was just like them. When they went back to their hotels, though, they wrote about him in their notes, and feared and worried that there was such a stranger in the world, and wondered whether the genes in the lower part of his body were different from those in the upper part. Italians came over and shook hands. His fellow Brazilians did all of the above. Some of the Catholics crossed themselves. His favorite was the man who took pictures. He'd gone toward the man the second time he came around but the man thought it was to do some violence and ran; but actually it was to ask for a copy of the picture of himself. It had never occurred to him to have anyone take a picture so he could see how he looked in the world.

"I must be a monstrosity."

"A monstrosity? You're a handsome fellow. You talk about the women's surprise and fear. You've been surprised and afraid of yourself."

"I know my mother told you about the healing nonsense. I did try one thing since giving it up. When this happened, I tried to heal myself."

"But you couldn't."

"No."

"So since you can't heal yourself, you're really set on not healing others."

"It's a lot of what you Americans call baloney. It has nothing to do with the world today, with its lasers and men on the moon."

I rubbed Vaseline on my knees, then I gathered up my legs in a lotus posture.

"Some ignorant belief."

"If belief works, it can't be ignorant. At least that's how I figure it."

"Like all you Americans."

"What?"

"Your great philosophy, your only philosophy, you offer to the world: what works is good."

"What works can't be bad. Maybe what works isn't the only good, but how else can you judge good."

"There ought to be another way," he said. He leaned back onto his black elbows. The insides of his arms were ashy. I dabbed on the Vaseline and rubbed.

"Well, for instance," he said, "the Mona Lisa doesn't work and she's good."

He was arguing it, but now it was a different kind of work. But maybe there was only one kind of work.

"I don't know about the Mona Lisa."

He looked at me sideways. "What?"

"I think the bitch works. Sure the bitch works."

"What do you mean?" He was frowning, wary.

"All the gawkers. You were working, weren't you? You were working like hell."

He shrugged his shoulders, leaned back, and watched the gawkers. I'm sure they couldn't tell if he was smiling or sneering, because I couldn't.

"Anyway," I said as we gathered up the towels and lotions and headed back. "Anyway, *this* bitch worked."

"What do you mean? And incidentally, I don't like that word for a woman."

"Incidentally, I don't either."

"Then why do you use it?"

"Because I've heard it too much."

"Anyway, go on," he said. "Explain."

"I mean after they got through looking at you, they'd look at me and wonder."

"Wonder what?"

"What sort of woman I was."

"To be with me?"

"Yeah, that, and . . . like maybe I was hiding something too, maybe even more amazing."

"What could you be hiding? You looked pretty much to me like you were showing it all."

"Even you haven't seen it all, buddy."

"Then show me."

"That's the other 'American philosophy,'" I said.

He waited. He said later I was full of gag lines. And the gag line, he said, was another American characteristic. According to him, I was just chock-full of these little American characteristics, like a bonbon full of hazelnuts. And America, from the point of view of the Latins, was the greatest gag line of them all.

"You noticed how the Americans were gawking the hardest," I said.

"Yeah."

"Well, they were the ones who believed what they saw the least. You could show yourself off till doomsday, and you'd still have to prove you existed."

"Be quiet, woman, and come on and show me something good. You don't have to show me till doomsday, but you can show me all night long."

I didn't come back with the next gag but it was there. I did put one line in though. "For all your complaints about Americans, you and your mama certainly know the lyrics of a lot of American blues and rock tunes."

He was looking like he didn't know what I meant. But he did flex a muscle when I talked about his mama.

33

I can't remember their names: Alexandro, Arturo, Christophe, Joaquim? Clara, Christina, Dominica, Victoria? Umberto? But I'll have them as Joaquim and Victoria.

"This is Joaquim and his girlfriend, Victoria. This is my friend from the States."

"Are you from the States? I've been to the States, to Chicago. Do you know Chicago?" asked Joaquim.

"Everyone knows Chicago," said Victoria. "He came back calling everybody 'my man,' even me." She giggled.

"What part of the States are you from?" asked Joaquim.

"Ohio."

"That's a state?"

"Sure, everybody knows Cincinnati." Victoria. "That's in Ohio."

"Get off your high horse."

"He brought that back too. I can't say a word without being on my high horse. He rides his all the time."

"They told me I'd get lost in Chicago, but I didn't."

"You told me you got lost."

"Yeah, I did, but they found me, so that's the same as not getting lost. But take our country. We have a very generous country too. There's a lot of it. But there are places if you get lost here, they never find you. Don't even play hide-and-seek here. You stay unfound."

Thin moustache, thick black hair. He looks like everybody's

villain in every movie I've seen. I discover he's the son of the owner of the mirror factory where Ensinanco worked for a summer.

"I've even gotten lost in New York and they found me, but get lost here and you disappear for good."

"You can get lost in Rio," said his girl.

"You can get lost in Rio even when you know where you are." He laughed. "You're in good hands with Ens my man though. Ens, my man, I'm thinking of going into business for myself."

"Great."

"Yeah, I'm thinking of going into business for myself."

He looked at me. "I've been to a lot of places, but the human species is the same everywhere. That's what you learn." He stroked my hand. "Let me tell you something."

"He doesn't mean any harm," his girl said. "Look, Quim, you're making her uncomfortable, and Ensinanco's not too pleased either."

"Ens, he's the man, aren't you, buddy? You always set up a big fuss about nothing. When you argue, you've got to place your argument on a sound foundation, which means it's got to be about something. Let me touch this woman's hand if I want to. Allow me to do that. I just want to tell her something: Not to get lost in Brazil because they'll never find you."

"You've already told her."

"And when you fuss, fuss about something."

"Well, that's settled," said the girl. She took Joaquim's hand off mine and held it.

"On your high horse again. Thinking of going into business for myself, Ens, my man."

"And you tell Ens that every year."

"I'm thinking of it. Sure I am. It's not just idle talk. My pop rose from nothing."

"I've never believed that," said the girl. "You always have something to rise from. You can't make something from nothing."

"My pop rose from nothing. Me, I'm like elastic though; all I need to do is stretch out what I've got."

"Stretching thins."

"Listen to her. Go to Rio."

"I mean you've got to add to what you've got."

"Go to Rio."

His girl looked at me. "He really is a nice guy."

"Have you ever been to a mirror factory?" He stroked my hand again.

"No."

"Nice place to work, if you don't mind seeing yourself every day." He leaned an ear back and listened to the music. There were couples on the floor. "Do you samba?" he asked. "Or whatever the heck it is they're doing. I never know what it is they're doing; I just get out and samba."

"Doesn't everybody?" said his girl. "Come on, I'll samba with you, if I still know how to samba."

When they were on the floor, Ensinanco stood up.

"Come on," he said.

"Aren't we going to wait till they get back? Aren't we going to be polite?"

"I *am* being polite," he said, and guided me through the dancers.

Like everyone needs a bit of local color, right?

34

Encobierta examined my back. The crocodile skin was cured. It's since returned, but then it was all healed up. I've never been very mystical, but honestly I can't tell you whether the cure came from her medicinal plants or his loving touches the night before.

"Oh, it's done a fine job, hasn't it?" she proclaimed, hands on my bare back. She'd propped a mirror on the table and held one at my back ("We've got more mirrors than we know what to do with!"), so I could see how clear and smooth it was.

And it was a fine job—skin like new.

"I'll fix up a bag of it; it's good for other ailments too. Stomach problems, female problems, intestinal sluggishness."

"Oh, I know about intestinal sluggishness!" I exclaimed.

She laughed and held my blouse while I put my arms in. She was chewing something, what I thought before was gum but discovered was raw cactus. She carried pieces of cactus in cellophane in her pocket and every now and then would pop some in her mouth. I watched her through the mirror standing on the table. I glanced at myself, then glanced away.

"I'm going to be going soon," I told her.

"At first I thought you were, and then after we talked I thought maybe I was wrong. I thought maybe instead of the wayward woman going your own way I thought you were, that maybe you really had come to stay with him—that maybe you could be the woman to shelter—rescue him from heaven's punishment.

That maybe you'd come here to save him. I started thinking perhaps love could save him—some special love, you see. But now I realize he has to save himself.

"Speaking of the modern world, he's like some Jonah in it—he runs off and tries to pursue a destiny different from the one that heaven's picked for him—and so this enchantment happens. He laughs at me when he hears my talk. I'm no ignorant old country girl like he likes to believe. I lived in Rio before he was born; I've mingled with folks from the top to the bottom, and from the bottom zigzagged back to the top again. I know this country like my palm, and I'm not afraid of hot or cold in it."

She swallowed the wad of cactus, popped another one in.

"I tell him it's heaven's punishment, but I don't know whether any of that's true. I just know what I see. And what I see is that he's black all at the top and white all at the bottom. But what you see and only what you see can't help you heal yourself. What do you see when you look at ipecacuanha —inconspicuous, growing there like any of God's plants, but get her inside of you and what wonders."

I still hadn't buttoned my blouse. I was leaning back with my elbows on the kitchen table, listening. She came and buttoned it, then went to the counter and started chopping meat and vegetables for the stew. The smell of garlic and red pepper filled the room.

"And if it is true, it's best you don't collide with destiny. It's best you flee."

"I'm a stubborn colored girl," I said. "If you make it seem like I'm running from him, perhaps I'll stay."

She shook her head vigorously, chopped fresh beef.

"No, you won't be running from him," she said.

She turned to me suddenly, the cleaver raised.

Like any fictioneer, I tried to resolve the scene. "I'll be running from *you*?" I asked.

She looked down at herself, the cleaver, beef blood on her apron. She laughed. I laughed.

"No," she said. "All of us run after our own selves. I may seem like I stay in one place, but I'm running after Encobierta too."

"And when we see you we'd better look out!"

"You darn right," she said, the cleaver raised again, her shoulders jiggling.

She stopped laughing and stared at me a moment. I felt as transparent as air. I thought she was going to talk about me, but she didn't.

"You know, in the colonial times they didn't have any inns, not an inn in the whole country. Traveling people had to have letters of introduction if they were somebodies and they stayed at the big houses, but there weren't any public facilities the way they had in Europe. At least that's the way I hear it. We had this man who was staying here, a historian working on a history of Brazil. Knew more about my own country than I did. Said he came here to learn the truth about it before he wrote his book. He'd been to all the major libraries in every country where people had something to say about Brazil, which means he's been nearly everywhere. Brazil, he said, was his last stop before he wrote his book. That seemed a curious thing to me, that it would be his last stop instead of his first. But he was disappointed, you know, because he felt he still did not know the truth about it. I don't know why I brought up that matter. Maybe it's just that folks are always looking for one big truth, and maybe there are just a lot of little truths. But the thing about the inns was a nice thing to know, since I run one." She smiled. "And do my running *in* one. I suppose if you weren't one of the somebodies you just slept under the trees. Then they built their own shelter, if they decided to stay . . . This inn used to be one of the big houses. We renovated it, put in electricity and running water, made it modern. His dad and me. His dad's half Black and half Tupi Indian; that's called *cafuso*, the historian told me. Sounds like confusion to me. He's always off and about somewhere, like he's being chased, then's back here when he's a mind to. Me? I stay put. I'm like my plants. No, I'm like a root. Valerio—that's his dad—he's like a root too, though, but one of those magic roots that can pull itself up and plant itself wherever it wants to be. I used to be a gadabout in the old days, but now I like my surroundings and they like me I guess. I've got my healing garden in the back. I don't think of Ensinanco as any sort of root, though. I think he'll plant himself in Rio when he starts his engineering practice, come now and then like he always does. He's not a root, and if he's a plant I don't know what kind. He only thinks he knows which way he wants to grow. You can't grow up without growing inside."

When I told Ensinanco I was going, we had just made love and were sitting in cane chairs, eating mandarin oranges and fresh coconut. We dipped our whole hands into the coconut shells and fed each other.

"You'll be back," he said shortly.

"I don't think so."

"Yes, you'll be back," he said. He put a finger full of coconut meat into my mouth. I licked his finger. "Anyway, there's a place for you here. When you come back, I'll have started my engineering firm and I'll have a place of my own."

"Suppose she's right, suppose if you went back to being a curandero, this would cure up, you'd be all black again?"

He plunged his hand into the coconut shell, fed himself.

"I don't believe it," he said. "But anyway, I prefer to pat the bull by the horns."

"Take the bull by the horns."

"In Brazil, we pat it."

He waited for my gag line.

So I return to Catherine and Ernest to pat the horns of the bull, or to pat its balls. It's your choice.

36

"I am not a very talkative man," says the maker of straw chairs. "I do not talk for talking's sake. When I talk, I speak from the heart or from the teeth."

I stand and watch him work. Some of the straw chairs look like they were woven from the heart and others from the teeth. I start to buy two from the heart but change my mind. I buy one from the heart for Ernest, and one from the teeth for Catherine. I cannot decide which to buy for myself. You decide.

"I never talk about devils, never, never," said Encobierta.

We sat at the kitchen table, drinking ipecacuanha tea. My luggage was at my feet. Ensinanco had gone to borrow a car to drive me to the airport.

"Never. When you talk about devils, they appear. I talk about angels."

"Do they appear?"

"No, but sometimes I hear the flutter of their wings."

She placed a bag of the dried medicinal plant in the pouch of my overnight case.

"Do you feel your time's been wasted with him?" she asked suddenly, her eyes like a squirrel's.

"No," I said more sharply than I'd intended.

She didn't back off.

"Sometimes a woman should let the grass grow under her feet."

"I always slip on grass."

What was the American saying? About a rolling stone gathering no moss. I bet if you examined one under a microscope, you'd discover flecks of it. All those sayings, cliches in one language, something fresh in another. Like the Welsh for it's raining cats and dogs: it's raining sticks and witches' brooms.

We heard Ensinanco's footsteps and hushed as he came into the kitchen.

"Have you girls been talking about me?" he asked.

Encobierta winked at me. "You've appeared, haven't you?"

She scooted out of her chair, picked up my overnight bag. Ensinanco picked up the suitcase and we marched out.

I sat in the jeep saying nothing.

"When I first met you," he said, "I thought you were too quiet for an American girl. I thought all American girls did was talk and talk. I thought they were made out of chitchat."

I laughed, leaned over and kissed his jaw.

The sides of the road were tree filled.

"Aren't those trees you can get oil out of, what's the name of them?"

"I don't know the name of them. But you tap them like you'd tap a maple tree to get syrup out."

"Yeah. I read about it in this magazine. This woman ran out of gas, and she took her bucket, walked over to one of those trees, filled up, and had enough oil to drive home. Let's just call it 'gas-station tree.'"

"Okay," he said, pensive, like he wasn't really listening.

"I bet you folks have so many natural resources here you haven't discovered yet," I said.

Now I was made out of chitchat and fidgety like I had a burr in my pants.

"So long," I said, when we arrived and extended my hand, ready to board.

He looked at me like I was a crazy woman. He grabbed both of my shoulders, pulled me to him, and kissed me.

"Just think of me as one of those gas-station trees," he said, turned and walked briskly back to the jeep.

I thought of all the people who saw him but didn't see him.

He didn't wave from the jeep; he just nodded and turned onto the road.

38

"You're Catherine Shuger's friend, aren't you?"

I was standing at the cosmetics counter at Hudson's in downtown Detroit.

"Yes."

She took hold of my elbow and moved me a bit away from the counter where I'd been sampling Charles of the Ritz's perfumes.

"Hasn't she been committed again? Didn't her husband commit her again?"

Catherine was out for the weekend, but Ernest was taking her back to Ann Arbor on Monday. I had flown in from Madagascar—where I'd been working on a travel book—to spend the weekend with them, but I didn't want to talk about my friends to this woman. She was an attractive young woman, wearing a fox jacket, midi-length wool skirt, and Italian leather boots. To look at her you wouldn't think she was a busybody. I wondered what she'd be wearing if she had to trap the fox herself.

"Is it true what they say? That he goes and gets her every weekend and takes her out, and every weekend she tries to kill him. Is it really true?"

"I heard it was every month," I said.

"You mean you don't know either? Aren't you two close?"

"Which two?"

Her mouth fell open. She gathered herself. Her fingers massaged her throat. "You're close to them both, I assume."

"They don't let me get too close," I said.

Her other hand was still on my elbow. It was insistent.

"Come on, what's it like? What's it like? It must be a trip."

I took my elbow out of her hand.

"I've got to be going," I said.

Both hands massaged her neck, then one settled on her hip; the other played with the fur on her jacket.

"She doesn't give interviews, does she?" she asked, both hands on her hips now.

"Oh, you're a journalist? Oh, that explains it."

"I tried to do a story on her for the *Detroit Free Press*. She wouldn't talk to me and her husband wouldn't talk to me. And now you won't talk to me. What's your name anyway?"

"Buck Mulligan."

"That's a funny name for a woman. Oh, you're kidding. No, that's not your name. I remember who you are now. When I saw you with them and followed you, I thought I knew you. I thought you looked familiar. You're that Wordlaw woman; you're that writer. That novelist. You haven't had a novel out in years. I tried reading one of your travel books, but girl, I couldn't get through that monster. I always did want to ask you, What do you consider the difference between porn and . . . ? Look, I could do a write-up on you. I would *love* to. We haven't gotten any *juice* from you in years!"

"No thanks."

"Why not?"

"I don't give interviews either."

"Why not?"

"So long." I backed away.

"You can trust me."

I said nothing.

"What are you working on now? I hope it's not another one of those *Summer in New Hampshire* books. We want some *juice* from you, girl!"

"So long," I said again.

"Sure, be that way."

I went back to the cosmetics counter to try some cologne. When I glanced over my shoulder the girl was still watching me, standing against a rack of dresses, her little finger stuck in the side of her mouth. I wondered again what she'd be wearing if she'd had to trap the fox herself. Well, she looked as if she'd have managed to get the fur of *something*.

When I open the door, Catherine is standing over Ernest holding a glass sculpture, ready to bring it down across the back of his head. I scream and he jumps up. The glass crashes into the back of the yellow leather chair. Ernest and I stand watching Catherine, whose hand has crashed into the pieces of broken glass and is bleeding. Then she is sucking her fingers.

"Do we have any mercury?" she asks.

"Mercurochrome, you mean," says Ernest. "Mercury's poison."

Ernest bandages her hand, while I clean up the glass pieces. The sculpture was too big to hide. The only way it could have gotten into the house was for him to have allowed it.

When Ernest leaves, I ask her.

"How did this get here?"

"Someone mailed it to me," she said. "I had to sign for it and everything. Special delivery, kiddo. Do you remember when I was in my transparent period?"

"What?"

"Oh, you didn't know me when I was in my transparent period. Used to do all this sculpture folks could see through. That's when I still could use glass, well, safety glass. I had to switch to plastic. You should have known me when I was in my transparent period. Someone remembered. Anyway, how toxic is it?"

I try to think of all the vicious someones who could get into this act.

She stares down at her bandaged hand.

"Where's Ern?"

"Gone out."

"I didn't notice he went out. Where did he go?"

"Who knows? To air out."

I hold in my fury. I've attached myself to them. I'm stuck too.

"Is mercury really poison?" Catherine asks.

We have the same thought suddenly, but we both dismiss it. Poison him? No, in all these years she hasn't tried to, and statistics say that that's the most common way a woman does it. But Catherine isn't the common woman. And poison is too easy, too quiet, too full of internal workings.

She wants the spectacle—the sudden violent act. The anticipation of blood. She is the French woman I saw in Marseilles eating the plate of raw hamburger, a raw egg on top, and fries and not comprehending when I told the chef that I wanted my meat without blood. *Pas rouge.* Without red.

Bien cuit. Tres cuit. Well done.

"Well done? Does that mean without blood?"

She wouldn't attempt anything that was without blood. Or without theater. It had to be theatrical, even if I was the only fool in the audience. Always the anticipation of the final scene. And the final scene was always murder. And like the Marseilles woman, she couldn't comprehend murder without blood.

"Poor beef, all juice gone. You no like blood? Blood good for you. Blood builds blood. I no like meat without blood. I no understand meat with no blood."

39

She's sitting across the table from me, sketching my shoulders—a study for some new piece she's working on.

"Undo your blouse some."

I undo it some.

Catherine's eyes are green. Today I wish they were darker. Today I feel they are not dark enough.

"Tell me about the last one who called you darling," she asks.

I laugh. "No one ever called me darling."

"No one ever? I can't believe that. Someone must have. Should I call you darling?"

"Of course not. Don't be silly."

She sketches. Pauses. Watches me. Rats' eyes? Chameleons'?

"Ernest called you darling once."

I frown. "He's never called me darling."

"Yes, he did. That morning. That morning when he brought us that basket of pears."

"He called you darling. He said, 'Darling, how are you?'"

"And then he looked at you and called you darling too. He said, 'Darling, how are you today?' He called us both darling. Well, someone's called you darling."

She sits with her arms folded, a Cheshire cat. Her smile lights up her face.

"No, he didn't call me darling, Catherine. Now I remember. He called me *doll*. I remember now. He called *you* darling. He said to me, 'Doll, how are you today?' He said doll."

Catherine frowns, leans into her drawing again.

I remember now, because I was thinking I'd never been called doll before. That was the first time any man had ever called me doll. I remember it, because I'd never liked the word doll for a woman, and somehow when he said it I liked it. Almost. But I didn't really feel like a doll. And it confused me that I almost liked it. I was too much flesh and blood to be any doll. Women who seemed like dolls frightened me.

"Bullshit!" she screams suddenly, throwing her charcoal pencil down. "He did too call you darling! Bullshit if he didn't. I know what I remember!"

"Catherine, you remember what you remember, I'll remember what I heard."

We sit watching each other, like wary foxes.

Then she giggles.

"Kiddo, I think this is going to be good."

40

When Ernest returned to the apartment, Catherine pulled some shit.

"Get out!" she screamed as soon as he entered. "Leave me alone with my woman. Don't disturb me and my woman."

Neither Ernest nor I expected that one. I just stared at her and Ernest stared at me. Finally, I looked at him. He walked into the kitchen, poured himself a cup of coffee. I followed him in.

"Ernest, don't believe what she called me," I explained. "I'm not her woman. There's no shit like that going on here."

"Sure, I know Catherine," he said.

"I don't know what got into her this time. You know there's nothing . . . You know how she likes to startle us by saying impossible things."

"Sure, I know," he said.

I poured myself a cup of black coffee, sat across from him. I felt like a leaf.

"That woman," I said, trying to laugh her off.

"Sometimes, though, I wish *you were mine*," he said softly, so softly I could have pretended I hadn't heard.

"No, you don't," I said, my eyes as wide as a rabbit's.

We watched each other for a moment, then I got up from the table.

Catherine was back in the studio wrapping her soul in flypaper. Her "soul" was what she called her favorite paintbrush. She had started to paint her sculptures deep, rich colors—turquoises, maroons, lavenders. The Egyptians, she said, painted their sculptures. It was one way to preserve the wood. "You didn't know me when I could use real wood," she added.

"Did you explain to him?" she asked.

"Yeah."

"I don't know why I said that dreadful thing," she said. "Yes I do. I wanted to make him feel like he makes me feel."

"How does he make you feel?"

She'd said "small" one time; maybe she'd give another story.

"What are you, a fucking shrink or something? Why don't you go and put him on your fucking couch? That's what you're aching to do, anyway isn't it? I heard."

How could she have heard what I scarcely had?

"I heard him call you darling that time."

"You *misheard*. He called me doll and it was playful and there wasn't any . . . Anyway, you were chattering away so. You chatter so much you don't listen. But Oz for us if we don't attend to every dot and dash you say! What the fuck? I'm going out myself."

She was the leaf now.

"You're coming back?"

She stood with her neck stretched forward like she was a turtle peeping out of its shell and trembling at the world it saw.

"Sure I'll be back, doll," I said, and walked out.

41

A basket of fresh pears. He put them on the breakfast table, kissed Catherine's forehead. "Good morning, darling." Then to me, "Doll, how are you today?"

"You're all bright and chipper," said Catherine, her eyes the color of the pears.

She picked one up.

"I love pears when they're hard. I never liked a soft pear. Ern likes his mushy. I love hard pears, hard apples, hard peaches, but you can't hardly ever find a decent hard peach."

Ernest opened the newspaper and I brought out the bread, jam, and olives.

That's how I remember it, anyhow.

42

I stare at the ocean, holding sand in my fist. Catherine and I are two beached whales, fattened from milk and soda crackers. I let the sand run through my fists. On the biggest hill one can see the church fortress. Built some other treacherous century when they were perpetually fearing invaders from the sea. Military or religious? Anyway, when its military uses were done, they'd worship. Pristine gray stone. Its uses gray. Ambiguous. In its doorways, you'd not know whether to expect a priest or a soldier. Let Catherine describe it architecturally. To me, everything is gothic.

"Do you think we're at the center of it?" Catherine asks.

"Of what?"

"The world."

I shrug and smile. I have always felt at the edges of it. Postcards are easier than worlds. But even there, picture me the sleepy face in the margin, half in shadows, but always watching.

"Do you feel like you're in the center?" I ask.

"You always feel like you're in the center wherever you are," she says.

Then let it be true for some of us.

Catherine is sitting on a large dry log and I'm sitting on a hill of sand.

"Do you ever think you'll go back to your husband, your Lantis?" she asks.

"No, I don't think so."

In one of the African countries they have a saying: Can you look the crocodile in the face? The crocodile is your own past. Right now I can only look at the crocodile from the corners of my eyes.

"But *think* is not sure," she says.

Catherine struggles up a hill of sand. She's wearing yellow cotton shorts and a yellow sweatshirt. The muscles in the backs of her legs are bulging. I imagine from the front that her chin is rippling. It's going double.

A seagull squawks. Catherine turns suddenly and watches.

"I wish I were a seabird," she says.

We stand staring.

"But everyone wants to be free," she says. "But some birds are flightless, too, like the ostrich, or the emu of Australia. Some birds are as earthbound as we are."

At home, we sit in two peacock chairs. She is making a rug out of scraps of colored material and I sit listening to the radio.

"Basque homeland and liberty . . . they are getting hungry and will soon come down from their camps in the hills . . . it is an almost impossible task to wipe out terrorists completely . . . violence has flared up once again . . . no convincing explanation for any of this . . . many people are perplexed . . . they've grown used to having things their own way."

"You like having things your own way, that's why," she says.

Then Catherine is suddenly sitting there, looking like a Mayan laughing head.

"What is it, what's funny, what's the joke?" I ask, turning down the radio some.

"I was thinking about this woman. There was this woman in our neighborhood, crazy as a june bug. She used to steal dandelions from all the neighbors' yards so she could make her own wine."

"Dandelions are free."

"She was always high. She was always crazy."

"Everybody has a neighbor like that."

"You should have heard the way people talked about her."

But Catherine, nothing to fear, we do not live in neighborhoods anymore, so nothing to fear:

There goes Miss Catherine again after Mr. Ernest.

What?

There goes Miss Catherine again trying to kill her husband.

What's she got this time?

Poker in one hand and a broomstick in the other.

He running?

Yes, he's running. What man wouldn't run? Crazy as she is.

If you ask me, he's as crazy to put up with her this long. If it was me, I wouldn't stay with her. Lock her up, throw the key in the creek.

Naw you wouldn't. Not if you loved her you wouldn't.

If you ask me, some love is the dickens.

You know why I wouldn't ask you, because if he did up and leave her, you'd be the first one talking 'bout what a wicked man Mr. Ernest was. He wouldn't just be one devil; he'd be a troop of devils.

And what do you think about that woman that done moved in with them?

I haven't formulated my thoughts on that one yet. But she do wear her age well.

What do she do?

I believe she makes paper.

I think they need to work her loose. Too many cooks in that kitchen.

That bedroom, you mean.

Don't be devilish.

Still, I don't know what to think about a man who saddles himself with that.

I read music but I don't read people.

I read people but I don't read fools.

Hush.

Yeah. There's that bewitching woman. Slit up the back of her skirt.

I don't read rough music. She better turn her volume down.

" . . . mixed with the vicious African strain."

"What?" Catherine looks up.

"They're talking about the killer bees," I say.

"Change the channel."

I change it trying to find music, but indeed there's more news, or more talk.

"I don't really keep up that much with what's going on in the art world. It's my own monsters I worry about."

"Keep it there," says Catherine, her eyes suddenly bright and wary.

"That's Gillette, isn't it?" I ask.

"Hush."

We listen. The interviewer had asked her something we hadn't heard.

"Uhm, yes," she was saying.

"You've disappeared for much too long. Everyone out there should go see her show; it's a 'big flight.' The name of it's *Flight*, folks, and it's a big one."

"She's not here?"

"No, this radio is one of those international kinds, picks up New York, Monte Carlo, Paris. She could be anywhere. I think this is a New York channel, though."

"They tell me you've started painting with something unusual. Tell me about it."

"Uh, they must have told you I painted those pictures with, uh, wild mushrooms because I, uh, like the texture."

I can picture her pushing her pale hair behind her ear. I look up and see Catherine pushing her hair behind her ear, though it's too short to push. She seems to have edged toward the radio, though in reality she hasn't moved.

"When I use different things for brushes I, uh, feel like I'm in new territory, exploring new territory. But I've stopped using the mushrooms because, uh, it's difficult to talk about but I have to tell the people why. You see, this one day I, uh, had this basket of wild mushrooms sitting in the studio on a stool and Tatum, that's my daughter, wandered in and ate them. I don't know why she did it because she's seen me painting with them before, and I've explained to her. But I'd had to go out for a while, and when I came back there she was, uh, eating them like . . . the mushrooms were poisonous you see . . . I'd explained to her . . . And there we were, staying in this place with just one telephone, this little town in Mexico. I'd gone there to try to get back to work again, to real work, you know? This place had just one telephone and I ran with her all the way . . . If she hadn't eaten the whole basket . . . I felt like a real bastard."

"There was nothing you could do. The folks understand."

"She'd seen me painting with them before, and I explained that they were the kind that couldn't be eaten."

"It must have been devastating."

"It was."

"But as I was saying, the art world is certainly glad that you've reemerged with your fantastic imagination . . . This is really a sexy show, folks, excuse me, erotic . . . Dali with *juice*. You're wild, and I say that in the nicest way . . . And you should see her, people, the same beauty we remember."

"Thank you."

"Why were you in Mexico?"

She snaps. "I told you: so I could get my work done. I also wanted to be there because I'd been studying Aztec art. You see, I like to mingle non-Western effects in my work. I like to, uh, so to speak, hang out around the work of primitive artists."

"You've got some really wild colors, wow. I can see the influence. With you on the scene again . . . Well, let's say modern art is in for some surprises . . ."

Catherine grunts and shrinks down in her peacock chair. The rug, looking like a coat of many colors, stares up from her lap.

"The poor little girl," I say.

She looks at me; surprise and rage.

"*She* did it."

"What are you talking about?"

"*She* killed her."

Catherine leans forward and drapes the unfinished rug around her shoulders.

"Catherine, I can't believe that," I say.

"It wasn't an accident. She left them there so Tatum could get them, because she knew Tatum would see them and couldn't keep her hands off of them."

I shake my head.

"I can't believe that."

Catherine sighs. "No one else'll believe me either. I could tell the whole fucking world and they wouldn't believe me."

I rub my forehead.

"It's a marvelous show," the interviewer is saying.

"I don't believe that," I say.

"Uh, thank you."

"And she's still the same beauty, folks."

Gillette laughs.

"She knows I know," whines Catherine, "but she knows I don't have any way to prove it. No one would believe me. No one would believe me over *her*."

I keep rubbing my forehead.

"You never even liked her," says Catherine. "And even you can't believe me over her."

My hand jumps from my forehead to the back of my neck.

"You're magic. Gillette Viking, ladies and gentlemen. If you get a chance come and see the Gillette Viking showing. Well, it was an honor to talk to you after all these years. I think you're the strongest, the absolute best of your generation. You know that we of your generation have always expected a lot from you, and we're proud that you haven't disappointed."

Catherine shrinks down further in her chair: if she could have disappeared she would have.

"Uh, thank you," says Gillette.

Catherine pulls at the nappy edges of her hair, looking like a djinn has hold of her.

43

"When I was a little girl I didn't know how it was done. I used to puzzle over it."

"What?" asked Ensinanco.

I stroked the border where his navel was, the top midnight and the bottom dawn.

"How a woman opened up for a man so that he could enter her, so that a man could get inside. I mean how they made love. I couldn't get the geography right. I couldn't imagine how it was physically done."

"A woman never opens up for a man; a man forces her open," he said, taking it out of the physical territory again.

"I don't believe that," I said.

"But it's true. A woman never opens up spiritually for a man to enter. Certainly no woman has ever opened herself up—opened her spirit up for me. At first I thought you might. But now you're leaving and going back to the States people."

"States people, ha; I've never heard us called that before."

Now I am going back to Catherine and Ernest, the States people.

"Has a man ever gotten your spirit open, and gotten in, really gotten in, and mingled his spirit with yours?"

I didn't answer. But he got my body open, at least, and he's inside dancing.

"I could just keep holding you," he said.

"And what about a man? Does a man ever open up for a woman?"

"That's not a man's nature."

"You're kidding."

I tickled his navel.

44

But Ensinanco's too mystical. I do not want to tell stories of heaven's punishment, or abandoned healing powers, of modern-day Jonahs running in the world. I want to tell of everyday people, like you and me.

There's that Malagasy time. There's Vinandratsy and his wild-flower sister, Miandra.

I sat on the long porch of his cattle ranch, on a wicker sofa. He had given me a raffia fan and I was fanning away flies with it.

"You're quiet for an American woman," he said.

I laughed because I'd heard that joke before.

"Did you think we were all made up of chitchat?"

His sister, Miandra, who lived with him, did not like me on sight.

"It's not you she sees," he explained. "It's any American woman."

"Any American woman?"

"She thinks all American women are rakes!"

45

I stood at the flower seller's stand admiring the orchids. Suddenly there was the smell of something like saddle soap, and I turned to stare at the most beautiful brown eyes. I had asked the flower seller in French why one orchid was more expensive than the other, but my French was a very formal, book-learned French, my American accent very thick, and she hadn't been able to understand. The man started explaining. I do not remember the names of the orchids, though he named all of them by the individual names—giving the Malagasy, the French, and the English names for them. I'll just have to call them "this girl" and "that girl."

"This girl, though she's prettier than that girl, is cheaper because she's the easier to find. She grows just about anywhere. Now that girl, you only find in the mountains and it's hard climbing to get to her, so she's very precious and very expensive. This girl can grow just about anywhere, but she always surprises you, you never know exactly where she'll pop up—her price never stays the same. When she's plentiful, she's cheap; when she's full of her tricks and games, she's expensive. And this girl here grows only on the barest mountaintop. You take the hardship to climb up there and you never know whether you'll find her at all. You may spend weeks looking for her, gathering lesser flowers, and then, all of a sudden, when you're least expecting, when you're not even looking anymore, you turn around and there's the beauty!

But it's a beauty—not a flashy beauty but still a beauty some might overlook until they know how hard it was to come by."

One believing any beauty in the world was hard to come by could hardly say no when this beauty invited me to have a drink with him in the hotel lounge.

"Are you her orchid salesman?" I asked when we had settled. "You know them so well."

"No, I'm a cattle rancher."

Saddle soap. Mixed with the smell of brilliantine. His hair glistened.

"I should have thought of that," he said, and sprang up suddenly. When he came back he was carrying the orchid that was the hardest to come by.

Sweeten me up, fill me with delight, and swallow me whole.

"How did you get to be a cattle rancher?"

"My family's always been cattle ranchers. Well, not always. My sister will tell you when we were princes and princesses." He smiled, then frowned. "Me, I think I'd rather be an orchid finder."

"I think I'd rather be that too."

"What do you do?" he asked.

That question always made me do a somersault and try to come up standing. I would never say as easily as some "writer." I was no longer a housewife. I once told a fellow I was a "limbo expert."

"I'm a limbo expert."

"We're all limbo experts. What else do you do?"

"I'm a freelance journalist. I was assigned to do this article on the flora of Madagascar for this gardening magazine. But I guess you already know how little I know about Flora, or her sister for that matter, and how big a bluff I am."

The rest of it's silly, I guess, when you read it on paper. Like the fellow telling the woman he'll teach her everything about Flora and her sister, from A to Z, but they'll start with C. Why C? she asks. C for Come home with me, he says. Filled up with brandy and beauty she says she will, and so after he gets through with his business in town, she packs her bags and follows him to his ranch. His jeep smells like saddle soap and brilliantine, a smell that has begun to seem comfortable and loving.

"That's a nice mountain. I've always loved mountains. I've seen all kinds of mountains and never been in one."

"Well, we ought to do something about that. That one's got a history that might interest you. It's sort of a mystical mountain. In the seventeenth century, I believe, fugitive slaves and pirates used to hide out there."

I wondered what fugitive slaves and pirates had to do with mysticism, but I didn't ask.

"What's its name?"

"You'll have to ask Miandra; she's the one who keeps up with the names of mountains, not me."

"You know the names of all the orchids in the world, and you don't know the name of one little old mountain."

He laughed, and I drew closer.

"So who's Miandra?"

If you've ever seen a cat hump up, that's Miandra when the jeep drove up. She was sitting on a porch swing fanning. The fan stopped. She got to her feet and stood looking. If you've ever seen a cat humped up and snarling, you've seen Miandra, except the snarl was invisible and covered the prettiest mouth you've ever seen.

I laughed her off but still felt uncomfortable around her. She was like a cat all right. She didn't fight those she didn't like. She moved around them with indifference, but cognizant indifference, if you can picture that. She looked at me as if I were a hole in space. If Vinandratsy came too close he would fall in. It wasn't possible for any American woman—even one as dark as she was—to be anything but a danger in the world.

She was a woman of thirty, refined, intelligent, and still a maiden I learned later. Her hair was black and glossy. She had a boyfriend who had not gotten beyond stroking her neck and watching her purr. He would come and sit in the parlor with her, holding his straw hat on his knees and glancing at her out of the corners of his eyes.

"He's her fiancé," Vinandratsy explained. "He loves her, but she doesn't love him at all. She tolerates him, that's all."

"That's an awful thing."

"But it's true. The others, there were plenty of them, they've stopped coming, married other girls—but he persists."

Once I was standing against the corral fence watching a herd of zebu and English cattle and her fiancé came up beside me, and we stood together watching, silent at first. He seemed to be waiting for me to speak first, so I did.

"Are you a cattle rancher too?" I asked.

"No, I'm an exporter."

"Of what?"

He seemed a bit ashamed, like he wasn't sure I'd think it was much.

"Vanilla beans."

"You smell like vanilla," I said readily.

That seemed to make him comfortable and cheery.

"You and Vinandratsy are becoming close," he said.

"We're becoming friends," I amended.

"Yes."

"Miandra doesn't like me though."

"No," he agreed. "But as for me, I think Vinandratsy has a right to such a woman."

I stared at him.

"You know, Miandra doesn't like me either. Oh, I guess she likes me, but she doesn't change. I've known her since she was a girl. Haven't you ever seen such a beauty in the world? Such a beauty that threatens a man with pleasure?"

"Threatens?"

"Ah, pleasure is a dangerous thing, didn't you know that?

There's no escaping such a woman. I persist, and she'll give in to me one day. One fights for such a woman and then one pays for her."

"Don't wait too long," I said. "And don't pay too much."

I looked away from him at a zebu cow standing beside an English bull.

"But I'm a prattler," he was saying. "Vinandratsy says I talk just to hear my own words."

But I'd never heard him talk much. I'd never heard him say one word sitting beside her, holding his straw hat in his lap and looking like a big bear in armor. She'd throw him indifferent glances while she'd fan herself with this antique raffia fan, though the house had air conditioning.

46

At the kitchen table, Vinandratsy and I sat examining maps. Miandra stood at the stove making a tea out of scorched rice, something for us to take on our journey. It was supposed to give energy and be more refreshing than ordinary tea or water.

Vinandratsy began telling me what I should wear. We were going into the mountains to see a place where pirates and fugitive slaves once hid out. Now there was barren rock and a few scattered mountain villages. But I still wanted to see it for myself and include a description of it in my book. And there was a certain orchid that grew only in that barren region.

"She knows what to wear," said Miandra coldly. "You don't have to explain every little mite to her."

"Darling, Amanda says she's never been in the mountains before."

"Yes, she has," fussed Miandra. "They have mountains in the U.S.A. They have plenty of mountains in the U.S.A."

"I've never been," I said. "I've seen a lot of mountains, that's all. I've never been in one."

She grunted, stirred the rice tea. She had browned the rice and then strained it.

"You see," said Vinandratsy.

She grunted again. "Well, I hope you don't get lost. Vinandratsy has no sense of direction. I hope he doesn't take you all over the damn mountains before you find the place you want."

She put the rice tea into thermos bottles, then made beef sandwiches.

When we were ready to go, Vinandratsy kissed Miandra's jaw.

I nodded to her. She looked at me a moment, then said, "It used to be called the holy mountain, but it's not holy anymore."

"Some of the mountain people still believe it's holy," said Vinandratsy.

"What they believe doesn't count anymore. Not in today's world."

Vinandratsy shouldered the backpack. Miandra stood in the doorway, waving at us, her forehead painted with sun.

In a moment, she was running after us holding out a little jar.

"Here, you forgot this," she said to Vinandratsy. "You don't want the anopheles mosquitoes to eat the girl alive."

She handed him the jar. "Well, she looks like she's been in plenty of mountains to me, but you show her how to use this concoction, Viny. Just a little bit goes a long way. I'm sure it's just the mosquitoes she wants to frighten off."

It's talk like that that makes you want to salute, but of course you don't dare.

47

"Do you still believe it's holy?" I asked, as we lay in sleeping bags against a crag of gray rock. The stars were so bright and near in the black sky that they seemed as if they'd been painted on.

"Yes," he said. "I still believe it's holy."

He unzipped his sleeping bag and came into mine.

He dotted my forehead and behind my ears with the insect concoction. He dotted himself.

"It doesn't have any odor," I said.

"To us it doesn't, but if you were a mosquito, you'd head for the other mountain."

We made love and then I closed my eyes and dreamed. We were on the same mountain, but I was someone else and he was another: and he was whole—the bottom of him as dark as his top. We were both wearing shirts and trousers, and though I had no X-ray vision like Superman's, I knew he was whole, that he had healed himself.

We were both on guard duty. I wore trousers, but I was still a woman. The fugitive slave women were warriors too. A strange conversation we had, the sort of conversation that one finds in dreams, and that would speak for madness in the real world.

"Shall you be here?" he asked.

"Yes. I'll spread my wings and wait for you."

But he stayed standing beside me, and we watched a ridge of traveler's trees.

"Don't puff up with too much pride," he said, "because in a world of blind women, a one-eyed woman only appears to see."

"What about you fellows puffing up? I'm not here to humiliate you, you know, but when we're in camp it seems like all you do are little things to humiliate me in front of the others. You won't even ask us women whether we approve of the plan?"

"Do you approve of the plan?"

"Yes, but you always do as you see fit. Do as you please and take your amusement at us women's expense."

"War is no amusement, and it's always a man's expense. Don't badger me with a molehill when we've got a mountain to fight. If they capture us, it's our lives. What becomes of you women? You're treated like flowers compared to us!"

"Flowers crushed at the heel. They'll humiliate us too. We'll move from one humiliation to another."

"What humiliation?"

"Oh, why don't you just pack me in straw and ship me off?"

"I love you."

"Well, we protected ourselves the last expedition. But what I say is don't rejoice once you've got over the devil's back, because you might just find yourself under his belly."

"Let's don't argue. Let's just watch out for *them* . . . Don't you know how well I think of you? I probably think better of you than you think of yourself."

I feel like I'm being lifted up. Someone is lifting me up in the air.

I wake up before I find out whether I'm being lifted up to be made love to or to be packed in straw.

"Where do you go next?" he is asking.

We sit with our backs against rocks. It is morning, and we are drinking rice tea and eating beef sandwiches. He is eating beef sandwiches. I began eating one until I discovered it was made out of the hump of the bull.

We sit at right angles from each other.

"Is there any plan to your travels? Any scheme to them?"

"No. I keep things open. But first I'll probably return to the States. It'll take me three or four months to write this travel book up from my notes and pictures."

"But you're the kind of woman who likes to steer her own ship, like Miandra."

I want to say that I am hardly Miandra, hardly as vicious or self-centered; maybe as self-willed but willing what I hope are better things. And I wouldn't keep a fellow on a string for twenty years hoping for some dangerous pleasure that I couldn't even myself imagine.

I do not say any of this, of course, of the princess.

"But you are disillusioned," he says.

"What?"

"That's what I read in your eyes, some brand of disillusionment."

It is not disillusionment he sees but what Richard Wright would call "the defense of indifference." Perhaps I am as vicious and self-centered as Miandra. I am out in the world, merely, yes. But I still speak at what Paz would call "the other" from behind shields. And I'm always doing my book.

I wear my notes and pictures like a shield.

"Someone must have hurt you very badly."

"No."

"Tell me your story."

"I don't have a story to tell."

"Everyone has a story."

I look away from him and stare at the ridge of traveler's trees.

Nobody wrote about our little village before, this man told me once. Pilgrims just used it as a stopping-off place, to get to the place where they really wanted to go. Even pilgrims don't even come here anymore. So I wrote about his little village, to try to bring back the pilgrims.

"It's either disillusionment or bitterness," he says. "And women carry them both very badly."

I smile over at him, wanly, stretching only one corner of my lips. Inside, I am shrinking Catherine. Inside, I am a woman wearing a necklace of teeth.

"I thought they were the same thing anyway," I say.

48

"No, not those chairs," the hostess says. "They're not to be sat on. They're just to be looked at."

I stand eating cheese from a small china plate.

"You look like Nefertiti," the woman says, coming up to me. "My husband thinks so too."

She moves away, shoos someone else. "Oh, not those chairs, dears; they're only to be looked at."

Lantis comes up to me. "How are you doing?"

"I don't know why I'm here."

"Are you the husband?" the hostess asks. "I'll get you a drink."

"No thanks."

"Oh, you're a teetotaler, how nice." She glances around. "No, not those, dears. They're just to be looked at." Back to us. "Your wife, your wife, she's like a phantom. She read beautifully, but we can't get her to talk. I'll bet with you she talks and talks and talks, you can't hush her up, ha ha . . . Not those, dears, they're just to be looked at . . . She doesn't like us. We think she's beautiful, but she doesn't like us at all."

Lantis leaves us, comes back carrying my coat.

"Let's go," he says. He guides me to the door. Outside it's windy. He buttons my coat.

"We should go back and be polite," I say.

"Why? It'll keep them wondering about you anyway," he says. "It'll keep them a little frightened, keep you a little mysterious. Either that or they'll think you're an arrogant stuck-up bitch. Either way, they won't invite you back."

I frown. The wind blows me against him.

"But what we say is to hell with them, right?" he says, taking my arm.

"Right," I mumble.

He opens the car door for me and I climb inside.

49

There's a man talking to me. He stands gulping down gin. A bird's beak. A long chin. Hair as white as Hemingway's at fifty.

"Are you a professor here?" I ask.

"No, I don't do anything; I just like to go to parties."

He dips a cracker into melted cheese, offers to feed it to me. I shake my head.

"You were quite good," he says.

"Thank you."

"Actually, I teach Chaucer. Your racy dialogue reminds me a bit of his."

A woman brushes by him, pinches his arm. "Lafcadio, you devil, you never commit yourself to anything. We're still over here waiting for your opinion."

"Right now I'm committing myself to this glass of gin, and the shape of that woman's ass."

"Which one?"

"Over there." He points.

"Oh, you're no good; you're shameless." She giggles and flutters away.

He turns back to me.

"Smile."

I smile.

"Show me your teeth, I mean."

I show them, like a jack-o'-lantern.

"Did you know that a gap-toothed woman is a sign of a lecherous woman—in medieval folklore?"

"I'm not gap-toothed."

"Well . . . no, a piece of raisin."

He removes it with his finger, pops it into his own mouth.

I stare, unbelieving.

"Turn that music up, Harriet. That's Latin inspired. Do you rumba?"

"No."

"No?"

He lifts my hand. "You're married. Is your husband here?"

"No."

"You're wonderfully monosyllabic too, aren't you? Just like the old bard. *Awake anon.* Wake up, Woman! *Yis?*"

I bite into another piece of raisin cake.

"Excuse me, I'm going over here and get a closer look at that piece of ass. It's talking to me if the woman won't."

50

"This is shit," he said, laying the pages on the coffee table.

"It's shit?"

I stood in the corner of the study, feeling as cornered as the furniture.

"Yeah, you can't publish this shit," he said.

I said nothing.

"Is it that bad?"

"I think so."

I drooped like a wet rag. Then I took the proofs and put them in the desk drawer. I sat in the hard chair looking at the wall but not at him, though I could tell his eyes were on me.

"So what are you thinking?" he asked.

I said nothing for a moment, then it came out like a dam had broken loose. "I'm thinking of the women writers I know who live with men who think their work is shit, or next to shit. I can list about five of them. But I can't list any, not one, of the men writers I know who live with women who think theirs is less than fantastic."

"They're better liars."

"That's not true. That's not true," I said. Then I said, "They wouldn't put up with it. They wouldn't. Why do you think we women put up with it?"

He was silent. I glanced over to see his shadow to make sure he was still there. His shadow raised its arms over its head and yawned. One arm came down first, the other looked like it was saluting, then it fell to its knee and scratched.

"Am I boring you?" I asked.

"Go on Manda-Panda, what's up?"

"Maybe all of our women's work *is* shit, let's suppose, but I'm sure all six of us could find at least some man who thought our shit was taffy."

"I'm sure you could," he said.

"Suppose I thought you were a lousy biology teacher?"

"But I'm not; I'm one of the best."

"Suppose I thought you were the worst?"

"But you don't."

"Of course I don't. I think you're great. But suppose I didn't. What would you do?"

"I'd put your ass out."

"You're joking, but that's exactly what you would do. You'd put my little ass out. Correction: my *big* ass."

"Seriously, Manda-Panda . . ." His shadow shook its head, shifted on the couch.

"I am being serious. And don't call me Manda-Panda except under conditions of confessions of love. Excuse the bad form."

"Seriously, Amanda, I'll be embarrassed for you if you publish that. I don't see how your editor . . ."

"You'll be embarrassed for you, you mean. For yourself."

"Yeah, I guess for myself. For the both of us. But wouldn't you be embarrassed for the both of us if you sat in on one of my classes and I wasn't quite up to snuff?"

I wanted to laugh at his old-fashioned way of putting it, but I sat with my eyes glued to his shadow. It ran its large hand through its thick hair. It yawned again.

"We'd be embarrassed for ourselves and for each other because we know we're capable of better," he said.

His shadow rose up and came to embrace (I started to write "embarrass") my shoulders.

"There's my lovely woman," he said, ready to call me Manda-Panda again, ready for kisses.

"Yeah, you'd put my big ass out," I protested, "but I bet you'd fuck it good first!"

I twisted out of his embrace.

"Stop this nonsense," he demanded. "Just stop it, Woman. Come to bed."

My feminist friends would be disappointed at the resolution of this scene, but I stopped the "nonsense" and went to bed, ready for kisses my own self.

51

Once Catherine sent me this picture postcard with a woman in white face and wearing a joker's cap—a sentimental clown. You've seen them. She scribbled "Self-portrait." She'd drawn the joker's cap herself, or painted it on.

52

Like I was sitting in this restaurant in New York once—Horn and
Hardart's I believe—and this man and woman were in the booth
behind me. I didn't hear the full context of the conversation, just
that suddenly the man said, "You clown." I waited for the woman's answer. Her voice when it came, was too soft, as if she still
had her milk teeth.

"I'm not what you think I am," she said.

He slurped his tea, laughed at her, and assured her she was.

She came back with the only defense she seemed to have.

"Don't slurp your tea," she said. "You're not supposed to slurp
tea; you're supposed to sip it. Slurping's bad manners. Weren't
you ever taught?"

53

"I wonder what it was like for them up here?" I ask.

"Who, the slaves or the pirates?"

"No, the women fugitives. Were there women pirates too? I guess there must have been, mustn't there?"

He looks at me as if the questions are too strange to answer. I cannot see his face in the dark, but I imagine that's his look. He turns over in the sleeping bag and goes to sleep.

I wonder if the place is haunted by the ghosts of the women, fugitives and pirates, but I am no mystic; all I see is the tapestry of stars and the shadows of giant boulders. I stretch out against his back and throw my arm across his belly. I smell the smoke from a Frenchman's musket. Slave catcher? Pirate? On the next cliff there's a row of traveler's trees.

"No paradise for a woman," he mumbles.

No paradise for a woman, but no paradise for a man either.

"Why do they call them traveler's trees?"

But he is silent. I must make my own answer. But are not all trees traveler's trees? Places to seek rest, the only places where any traveler's welcome.

He reaches his hand back, presses me nearer him. I kiss the back of his neck. He turns to me and we make love again.

"I can hear the wheels inside you turning."

"What?"

"I can hear the wheels inside you turning."

"Is that your way of saying I'm the mechanical woman?"
"The original."

But it is a dream, and I am really sand poured through fingers. I am really sand. I am really sundial and magnolia blossoming.

54

We sat at the back of the restaurant, eating a Chinese dinner.

Shrimp and fried rice, sweet and sour pork, snow peas.

"Tomorrow, I'm going to Madagascar to work on a travel book," I said.

"Oh?"

"I've got my tickets."

"Why are you telling me now?"

I bit into a piece of sweet and sour pork.

"I wasn't going to tell you at all."

"That would have been pretty rotten," he said, his eyes narrowed and cold. Then he arched his eyebrow. "But why weren't you going to tell me at all?"

I stared at the gray in his moustache. He brushed his hair back with his hands. His forehead was a brown bell.

"Because I've decided I'm not coming back."

He put down his fork.

"Because of what I said about your book?"

I stared at his snow peas, his fried rice.

"That's ridiculous. That's childish. That's silly. Why do you want to give me a hard time?"

"I don't want to give you a hard time."

He said nothing, then, "I'm not letting you go."

I pushed away from the table, then I pulled my chair up to it again.

"How are you going to spend your time?" he asked. He had let me go.

"Working. Working on my book, like I said. Maybe you don't think that's much."

He sighed. He rubbed back his hair.

"What about Panda?"

I must say that I had not thought about Panda at all.

"She'll stay with you. I couldn't have her running about with me. She's too young."

"No, you couldn't do that. Have her getting in the way of your lovers."

I sat with my mouth open. I had talked about work, and he was talking about lovers. Well, I'd give him lovers! I'd give him work *and* lovers!

He straightened his tie, leaned toward me, his thumb on the corner of his chin, his knuckles riding his jaw.

"You're being ridiculous, you know?" he said.

I rubbed my arm.

"Yeah, I know."

Outside, he stood behind me, both hands on my shoulders.

"I can't pretend I liked your book. I can't lie about that. But I do love you, Manda-Panda."

I said nothing. We walked, holding hands.

"What are you going to tell Panda?" he asked.

"I'm not going to tell her anything."

He let my hand go.

"What sort of witch are you?"

But I had no gag lines, none.

55

"Do you want to come into town with me? I'm going shopping," said Miandra.

I was sitting in a corner of the dining room writing up travel notes, using the light from the window. This was the first time she had spoken so civilly to me. Gwendolyn Brooks has an expression—"civilize the space." For the first time, she had tried to "civilize the space" around us.

"Yes, I'd like to," I said, surprised and made awkward by her friendliness. I put the notebook down on the window ledge.

"That's not a diary too?" she asked.

"No."

"I was going to say, if there were personal things in there you'd better hide it. The girl is so nosy."

They had a servant girl from one of the mountain villages. She wore her hair in what looked like the sort of knots you see on trees. "Why do you wear your hair in that old way?" Miandra had asked once. Her name was Vahila. That's all I knew.

"Will Vinandratsy go with us?" I asked, as I stood.

"No." She frowned. "It's just us, just you and me. I hope you don't mind if it's just us?"

"No, of course not," I said.

I still stood by the chair, as if I were growing up from the floor.

"Sometimes I ride the mule in, but I bet you've never ridden one?" she asked.

"No."

"Then we'll take the jeep."

She was putting thin white gloves over her slender dark hands. The gloves were so thin you could see her skin through them—especially the darker pigmentation of her knuckles. She picked up her purse from the dining room table. The purse was one of those made of tan, Moroccan leather—made not with handles or straps but with a rectangular hole through the top where you put your hand through to carry it. I went into the bedroom and got my shoulder bag.

"Are you ready?" she asked when I came back in the room.

She had been standing looking out the window and turned from it when she heard my footsteps. I wondered momentarily whether she'd been looking into my notebook, whether it had been her own self she distrusted, and whether she suspected me of writing things about her, but both hands were clutching her purse.

"Yes," I said.

Outside I stood on the porch and waited while she drove the jeep around to the front, then I ran down the steps and climbed in.

"I've never learned to drive," I said, to make conversation.

We turned down a narrow road, surrounded by a forest of traveler's trees.

"It must make life difficult," she said. "I don't know what I'd do if I didn't drive. How do you manage?"

"I usually find someone who knows how."

"I'll bet you do. I mean, you'd have to, wouldn't you?"

She touched her jaw a bit. We passed a rice field. I saw several women in straw hats bending in it. Winnowing, cutting, threshing, gathering? What do you do with rice?

"You were right," I said. "That rice tea you made for us was very refreshing."

"Rice water it's actually called. I just say tea because you English say tea."

"I'm not English; I'm American."

"I know. I don't know why I said English. Yes, I do know why. Vinandratsy's last friend was English."

I said nothing but a butterfly jumped into my belly and started beating wings.

"Vinandratsy said you wouldn't eat the zebu sandwiches I made."

"I was going to, but he said it was made out of the hump of the zebu. For someone who travels as much as I do, I'm not good with international cuisine. I always chicken out."

"Chicken out?"

"I mean, lose courage."

"The hump's the best part. I hope you don't think I made you some scraps of pieces. In the old days, zebu's hump used to be royal food. Only kings and queens were allowed to eat it, but now almost anyone does."

"Oh, I see."

"You should be more adventuresome with food though," she advised. "I think you never really get to know a country till you explore its food. Of course it's easier to preach than it is to do. I bet you've never eaten grasshoppers, have you?"

"No and don't intend to."

She laughed. "You think you haven't. You gobbled that soup up last night and said it was delicious."

The butterfly turned into a caterpillar.

"It tasted like garlic," I said, matter-of-factly. "I thought it was turtle soup or something."

"I know you did. Vinandratsy kept asking you if you really wanted that. The Englishwoman ate it too."

The butterfly.

"Vinandratsy thinks he's done his part if he asks you if you really want it."

"Family joke, huh?"

"And it gets funnier. You got to know more about our country than you realize. Do you want me to tell you what else was in that soup?"

"No."

The look she gave me was inscrutable.

I stared into another rice field.

"The Englishwoman wasn't a bit amused either. She went back to Manchester."

I watched the trees.

She wore a long red silk scarf around her neck, which kept flying back, hitting me against the shoulder.

"But Vinandratsy and I are not just anyone, you see. We have royal blood running in our veins. One of the branches of our family can be traced back to Queen Betia. Eh, but it doesn't matter these days. Such things don't matter anymore. No one makes a fuss over royalty today."

I said nothing. Her long scarf flapped against my shoulder. We passed more traveler's trees, then fences, zebu and English cattle, rice fields. Perhaps that was why she was so tight with her soul, I was thinking.

Then I wondered why I had thought "soul"!

" 'Rice is life,' the kings and queens used to say."

Her long scarf flapped, struck my lip. I flicked it away with a finger.

"I'll give you a book on Queen Betia."

"Thanks."

Wildflowers, vanilla.

56

"When it was a kingdom," she said, glancing across at me and then back at the road, "there was more enchantment, but these days there's no enchantment in the world. Maybe passion must take the place of enchantment in the modern world, but sometimes I think there's no real passion either."

I did not answer.

"Maybe it's because I haven't discovered it," she said.

Her scarf hit me.

57

Returned from shopping, Miandra and I stood in the dining room. I was carrying some of her packages and started to put them down on the mahogany table.

"Come, let's put them in my room. You haven't seen my room."

I followed her into her room, a room full of light with a canopied bed, brocaded chairs, lace curtains, silk scarfs on the dressing table. A princess's room.

She put the packages she was carrying down in a chair and I followed suit.

"This is lovely. This is a beautiful room," I said.

"Thank you. I like this room too . . . Why didn't you buy anything?"

"I'm not much for shopping."

She smiled at me. "You didn't buy anything for you, so I did," she exclaimed. Reaching for the tiniest of one of the packages, she opened it and took out a necklace made of teeth. She held it up to my neck. I moved away slightly.

She laughed. "It's crocodile teeth. Some people still believe they're magic. In Queen Betia's day perhaps they were." She put the necklace over my head. "There. It looks beautiful on you. You look very beautiful."

She stood close to my face. I'm one who is stingy about my own space, so I backed away slightly.

"You seem a little nervous. You're not afraid of me, are you?"

I said nothing. She reached out and touched under my chin, straightening the necklace.

"It really looks nice. It looks nice against your skin."

She moved away from me and sat down on the bed.

"I'm tired. I'm going to take a nap," she said. "Aren't you tired? Why don't you come lie down with me? There's room enough for two people."

I looked at her clean, black, straight hair on the lace pillow.

"No, there's not," I said.

I smiled slightly. Her eyes were shining.

"Suit yourself," she said and stretched out.

I opened her door and went out.

When I was halfway down the hall, I heard her door slam. In the morning, she was back to her sullen ways again. There was no more "civilizing the space" around us. But she served only things I knew.

Book III   *Of Pilgrims,*
Self-Centered Bitches
(Peregrine Women?),
and Hard Nuts

58

Catherine is sleeping on the terrace in the lounge chair, leaning back, her mouth slightly open. Ernest goes over and touches her forehead and kisses her. She doesn't wake up, but the lines in her forehead deepen.

"Do you want to go for a walk?" he asks, turning to me.

"Will she be all right?"

"Let's go for a walk."

"Okay," I say, rising and putting my notebook on the table.

Ernest takes my arm and we go through the living room and down the stairs into the street. I glance back at the terrace, imagining Catherine awake and peering over the railing at us. But she's still sleeping, the sunlight in her hair, making ordinary eyes almost see the yellow aura.

There she is. Queen of the hill.

"You're a hard nut to crack," Ernest says, still holding my arm.

"What?"

"I've known you for years, and you're still like a perfect stranger."

On the beach, he puts his jacket down for me to sit on. He calls me "Pilgrim." I sit up, holding my knees, staring out at the bathers—multinational. Most of them are not swimming but sitting in the water. A white-haired Ibizan sits on a boat with "Charter" printed on a white, homemade sign on its deck. The white sails are rolled. Ernest stretches out, rests on his elbow, looks toward me.

"I don't feel I know any longer what's best for Catherine," he says. "This seesaw . . ."

"Are you going to put her away again?"

He stares at the sea.

"That's an awful expression," he says.

We're silent. I watch the man help a woman climb into the boat. A man in the water hands up her straw hat and straw pocketbook. He climbs up, without the aid of anyone.

"What are you thinking?" I ask Ernest.

"I'm thinking I don't know how I can spend the rest of my days like this. All these scrambled years. If you weren't in them . . ."

"But you love her. And you know that whenever she's . . . in the hospital . . . she won't work. You take her out so she can do her work too."

"And be dangerous."

I feel his hand on my cheek.

"It's time for us to go," he says.

"What?"

"You were sleeping."

"I slept?"

I raise up. "What time is it?" I see the sun sitting on the water. "Oh, no, why didn't you wake me?"

He smiles, takes my hand as I stand up. I lift his jacket, brush the sand off, and give it back to him, but he drapes it across my shoulders. We climb back to the road.

"Did you call me 'Pilgrim'?" I ask.

"What?"

"I thought that when we were on the beach, when we'd just sat down, that you'd called me 'Pilgrim.' I must have dreamed it."

"No, I called you 'peregrine.' Do you know what a peregrine is?"

"Yes. It's one of those birds that never stays in one place."

He is on the road first and reaches down to help me. I struggle on the loose sand. He catches my hand and pulls me up.

"Can you make it?"

"Yes."

When we're on the road, I hold his hand a bit more firmly and then let go.

When we return, Catherine is awake and sitting in the living room in a peacock chair. It is almost dusk outside. I don't know why, but I start explaining.

"We were down to the beach. I—like a fool—fell asleep. Ernest didn't wake me."

She says nothing. She stares at me.

"I've overstayed," says Ernest. "I'll see you two in the morning."

He stands in front of her as if he's about to kiss her. But she looks as if she doesn't know the difference between a bite and a kiss. He touches her knee instead. "See you." He goes.

"We only meant to stay for a little while," I say. "It's my fault."

"I'm thinking of going back," she says.

"He doesn't want to put you back," I say.

"I don't mean *there*." She rubs her forehead. "I mean back to the States. I'm thinking of going home."

In the dark, I'm sure I've turned purple. I stare away from her, then sit down in the other peacock chair.

"Do you think he'll want to go back?" she asks.

"Ask him."

"He thinks it's paradise here, but no place is paradise for me."

I stay silent.

"I'm the worm in the apple," she says.

"Oh, Catherine," I mutter, kicking my shoes off and leaning against the flared back of the chair—the peacock's lovely tail. "Don't think of yourself that way."

She turns on the table light. I stare at two eyes watching me, one's a comet and one's a moon. Her books on the shatterproof glass end table: *Art Now* and *The Last Magic*.

"I'm the worm, he's the apple, and what are you?" she asks.

What else could I be? I stand up and go onto the terrace where the television is, and a videotape of the World Series is playing. "Coke is it!" is displayed prominently above the batter's head.

59

Whenever Ernest touches Catherine, no matter with what de-
gree of tenderness, she shrinks from him. Now he is touching the
side of her face, and she is the shrinking woman.

Catherine's dress is canary yellow. Her sandals are high-heeled
and also canary yellow.

The three of us are on a narrow street standing against the
tall, white-washed wall of the cathedral fortress. I try to remember what is the difference between pure gothic and flamboyant
gothic. Is it that in one the stones seem heavy, in the other, light?
As Catherine walks, she runs her fingers along the white wall. I
imagine her, some medieval sculptress, hanging from ropes, chis-
eling stone.

Ernest walks in the middle. He just touched the side of her
face to remove a spot of dust from it (it was really makeup applied
too thickly) and she has shrunk from him. Now she is running her
fingernails along the wall.

Catherine's in her canary-yellow dress. I watch her dark pro-
file against the white wall. Suddenly Catherine stops walking and
leans against the wall, her eyes almost closing in the sunlight.

Ernest is wearing eyeglasses, the kind that darken in the sunlight, become crystal clear indoors and in shadows.

Catherine casts a shadow and they are crystal clear.

"I want to go back," Catherine says.

I know what Ernest is thinking. He is thinking what I was

thinking when she first said that to me. His breath rushes out. I cannot tell whether it is relief or alarm.

I want to save him from embarrassment or from something worse. I speak up.

"Sure; why don't we all go back to the States," I say.

Ernest's breath rushes in again.

"Is that what you want, Catherine?" he asks.

"Yes."

He nods. She moves to start walking again. Out of her shadow, Ernest's glasses darken. I think I can see his eyes behind them staring at me.

Catherine is upstairs napping in the peacock chair. Ernest and I stand downstairs in the storeroom where the trunks and boxes are. There is also fishing tackle and boating equipment left by the last tenants. The basement floor is stone.

"You're quiet even for you," he says.

"What?"

"Even for you you're quiet."

He touches my jaw. I am no shrinking woman. He kisses me, a short, tender one. He fingers the sweat along my hairline.

Finally, I move away from him, lift one of the boxes, and carry it upstairs.

When I go back downstairs, to carry up another box, Ernest has disappeared. I think about the Elizabeth Bowen story where the little boy believes that when one is not in the presence of certain people, they disappear, that they cease to exist in the world, and they only spring back into it when you're in their presence again. When you leave them, they disappear from the world again. For two days, Ernest does not spring into existence. For two days he has disappeared from the world. Or am I the one who has disappeared because he is not here?

60

On the morning of the third day, I walk down to the beach. Ernest is there, sitting on driftwood. When I call to him, he turns. He has a two-day growth of beard.

"Are you all right?" I ask.

I sit on my knees beside him. I touch his stomach and feel something rough through his shirt. I lift his shirt and find he's been wrapped in gauze.

"When did this happen?"

"A couple of ribs are broken, that's all."

"You should have broken hers. I'd have broken hers."

"No, you wouldn't."

I rise to go back.

"Don't go looking like that," he says. "Don't you go home with that face."

When we return, Catherine is sitting in her peacock chair, wearing the de Kooning Bicycle-Woman smile. I am wearing my ambrosia mask for Catherine. But I am in a floating world, and I cannot help but look at Ernest with different eyes, and Catherine cannot help but see it.

61

In the dream (we must distinguish our real worlds from dreams, though we live as long in one world as the other), I stood before the council of old men. I had done some wrong, somehow I had gone against the rules of the fugitive village.

A young man steps forward to defend me. I do not know who the young man is. His hair stands tall like a wild forest. He asks the old men why not issue me a warning first; he says that a warning would be sufficient, that they need not take more drastic measures.

"She is not the sort of woman to heed a warning," the old men say.

The young man tries to bring my merits before them: the bravery I showed in the last battle, that I fought as bravely as any of the men.

The old men answer that I used my magic; I bewitched them into believing I'd given a brave fight when actually I'd chickened out, turned tail and ran. Magic vapors from my medicinal plants made them hallucinate me brave.

"She intruded where she should not have," the old men say.

The young man says that it was merely words I gave them.

"Words we have no use for," say the old men. "Words that should never have been spoken here."

"Maybe it's possible that she didn't know that her words would have had such power to offend . . . Now that she knows . . . She'd walk on eggs . . ."

"That's just it. If she were a proper medicine woman her words would have *defended* us. We could have gone into battle armed with our weapons *and her words*. She bewitches us into belief in her when she's nothing but a harm in the world!"

The young man stands waiting beside me.

"Do you have a headache?" he whispers.

"Yes, and I'm nauseous too."

"Reach behind you."

I reach behind me. He passed the weed to me, and I pop it in my mouth.

"See, she chews her cud like a cow; she must be evil."

"Horned and hoofed," declares another.

"And that crocodile growth on her back pinpointed her for us. We didn't have to look any further when we found that. If she were a proper medicine woman she'd heal herself before making claims about what she can do for our daughters!"

"Bewitcher!"

"She's dwelt among us all these years," defends the young man.

"Since you had your milk teeth, brat. Out of here!"

The young man stays his ground.

"He's stuck on her, look at him! He's sticking to her like a beauty spot!"

"Or like ugly!" shouts another.

"Maybe we ought to banish that irritating fellow too!"

"No, gentlemen, that's just what he wants. The best punishment for this upstart would be to let her go and keep the bugger here!"

Guards come and escort the young man away.

"I suppose you had us hallucinate him too," says the chief of the elders. "You have no champions here! The terms of your punishment, Sancha, Bewitcher, are as follows: You'll be sent out of the village, down the mountain, a woman alone, and you know what that means, dearie."

"She knows what it means."

"If our enemies capture you . . ."

"She knows what that means. She can't hallucinate her way out of that!"

"Sent without food or drink . . ."

"Or clothing?"

"Oh, let her have the stuff; it's bark cloth anyway."

"Let her have the stuff; bark cloth anyway."

I rest beneath a traveler's tree.

"This the whole dream?" Catherine asks, approaching.

"Yes, this is the whole dream."

"And what happens after the traveler's tree part?" she asked, peering down at me, her finger stuck up her nose.

"I never get beyond the traveler's tree."

"Do you know what I keep expecting?" asks Catherine, leaning against the tree.

"What?"

"I keep expecting this traveler's tree to open up and take you in. Make a new home for you."

"Things don't happen that way."

"In dreams they do," says Catherine.

"Not in my dreams they don't."

"This must be some pretty pedestrian dream, girl," she says. "My dreams are wild; anything can happen. Anything is possible."

"Is *that* possible?"

"What *that?*"

"Is it possible, Catherine?" I badger.

She leans her cheek against the tree. "I don't like this dream. How did you get me into it anyway? I want out."

I shrug. "When a dream takes over, what can you do, kid?"

"If I were a traveler's tree, do you know what I'd do?"

"What? You'd open up for me?"

"Sure," she says, smiling. "I'd open up and eat you!"

62

Ernest and I sat across from each other in the peacock chairs.

"Your book on Bahian healers is quite nice," he said. "I liked your dedication too: for the healers."

"That means for you too."

"I haven't healed anyone."

"Well, you try."

"Everyone tries."

"No, everyone doesn't try either. Not at all."

He said nothing for a moment. He scratched his moustache. Had a smell like lavender and mint. He was wearing a dress shirt, but blue jeans.

"I like this a lot better than your fiction actually. It reads like fiction though. I mean the style is fictional, but there seems a lot more range. It's amusing and serious, almost surreal in places. And the healers are very interesting, as personalities. One seems almost mythical; his section read like a sort of fable." He shook his head. "I liked it a lot. And it's intelligent. I mean you can tell an intelligent woman wrote it."

"And not just a horny one?"

He frowned, stared out the window.

"That's what an article called me, a group of us. It was meant to be a joke."

"What, the article?"

"No, my saying that just now."

I felt embarrassed.

He said, "It's sort of in my area of interest, though it's not exactly what you'd call a *science*. But that psychokinetic stuff isn't really a science either. Borderline. Lasers in medicine, that's the future. But there are all sorts of forms of medicine that aren't official but that work. Still, it's healing with light; who'd have thought that? Sometimes I wonder what it would be like if it were easier for us."

"What do you mean?"

"If we could just take Catherine to a good witch doctor."

I laughed a bit.

"I know a woman who still believes in them," I said. "She went to one, said he healed her with music."

"Well, if that was all it'd take, Catherine would be the most healed woman!"

"You better believe it! This woman, though, said that he knew the right combinations of sounds. I think we just don't know the right combinations of sounds."

"Give us the right combination of sounds!" He raised his hands. He sounded like he was in somebody's church.

We laughed till our laughter itself sounded almost like some incantatory formula.

63

In Catherine's studio, we select and number sculptures—some to be shipped to New York to her agent and others to be shipped to their home in Detroit.

"I want to send this one to my agent," Catherine says.

"No, don't send that one . . . That's not anything yet," says Ernest. "Needs more work, don't you think?"

"This?" Catherine asks. Then, "Shall I ship this one to Detroit or to my agent?"

"No, none of those, Catherine, not to the agent. You want them to be good enough. I don't think they're good enough yet. What do you think?"

Catherine stands with her hands in the pockets of her yellow trousers. She stands squeezed in a corner. She mumbles something we can't hear.

"No, pack that one with straw," Ernest says to me. "That one has to be packed with straw. And don't touch this. I'll pack it myself."

"What about me?" Catherine asks suddenly.

"You?" Ernest turns and stares at her.

"I want to be packed in straw and shipped back too," she says.

"You have to speak up," Ernest says. "I didn't hear."

But Catherine can't speak up; she stands with her head tilted, looking idiotic, then she bends down and picks up *The Birdcatcher*.

I start to scream, "Watch out!," get my mouth into the "Wah," but she is bending toward a crate to deposit it.

I lift up a handful of straw and line the bottom of a crate. I pick up another handful.

"I'm not going back with you guys after all," I say, matter-of-factly.

Ernest has his back to me and doesn't turn around, though I see his shoulders stiffen. He goes on packing.

Catherine looks as if she's squeezed herself tighter into the corner. She scratches her bottom lip and stares at Ernest's back.

When she looks toward me, I feel like I've already disappeared.

The Stuffed Elephant

In a curio shop I buy a stuffed elephant.

"A leftover of the Republican Convention," the saleswoman says. "I didn't make beans when they were here. I thought I was going to rake up, but I didn't make beans. In fact I lost money . . . Are you a Republican?"

"No, I just like elephants."

When I come back to the apartment, my husband looks up, worried.

"Where have you been? I turn my back and you disappear."

He just stepped out a minute to go downstairs and get Coke from the machine. He didn't lock the door. Now he's looking at me as if I've got some weapon. I know he wants to search me, strip me down.

"I just went out for a walk. I saw this elephant and bought it. It's nice, isn't it?"

I show him the elephant. Its trunk is raised. Its little pink tongue is sticking out. I set it down on the coffee table. I know he wants to strip the elephant.

"A leftover from the Republican Convention," I echo.

He says nothing. He opens my can of Coke and hands it to me. Now he's staring at the tin can, wondering what weapon can be handcrafted from it. But the tin cans these days are too fragile. Anyone can crush them in the hand. No muscle woman.

Now he looks at me. I hate it when he looks at me like he doesn't know I'm Catherine.

"You want to give the talk, don't you?"

"Yes."

"I think you should. I think it will be good for you."

"Yes."

But when we get to the hotel, he leaves me standing in the hall, and goes to sign us in. I stand there in the corner hearing them.

"I bet she goes to pieces in there!"

"I love it! You know he got her out of the asylum in Ann Arbor. He took her out just so she could come here and give this."

"I don't think it's right."

"But they organized it before they knew the story. Shirley said she didn't know that Catherine Shuger was in such a condition. I asked her where she has been."

"I bet she goes to pieces."

"I wouldn't miss this for the world. She's been off and on again for years."

"I feel for him. I guess he knows what he's doing. Poor fellow."

"I think he's exploiting her."

"What would he need to exploit her for? You just don't know Ernest Shuger. She's the devil, not him. I just don't understand the man is all."

"The stuff she's doing nowadays, have you seen it?"

"Lord, yes."

"I remember just ten years ago . . ."

"I always thought she was the best . . ."

"I wish I knew where the *Black* was though."

"Don't you though."

"All that rage, we really expected something from her."

"Yeah, but we all thought we were the generation, though, didn't we?"

"Everybody does."

"I still wish I knew where the *Black* was."

"Is that her? Girl, you better hush!"

"Is that her? That's not her. That's not Catherine Shuger! She was such a beauty."

"That is her too . . . I remember we were all just awestruck by this fiery girl from Atlanta."

"Wasn't it Jackson?"

"No, Atlanta. This bright, intelligent, energetic young woman exhorting us all to build a better world."

"If that *is* her, you could cut bourgeoise with a knife."

"What do you expect, both her parents doctors? Well, you knew how she'd turn out."

"She told you that? She told me her mother was a laundress and her father worked in a tractor factory."

"Really? Well, she was one of the leading militants on campus. I guess it embarrassed her. All us grassroots girls. I found out one day when I came in to give her one of those financial aid packets and found out she wasn't even on financial aid; her parents had forked out the whole bundle, girl! Well, you know, in those days we were all trying to out-poor each other—not like the kids do now—out-poor and out-Black each other, like we thought our parents' generation were trying to . . ."

" . . . out-white each other! Girl!"

"She was a strange girl, though, all that rage and energy when she exhorted us at those rallies—then sometimes I'd visit her in her room when she was sketching and she was this really soft-spoken girl—child-woman—and you'd hardly know she was the same person . . . I mean that just doesn't look like her to me . . . Maybe that's her over there?"

"No, girl, I know who that is! I just came back from that reading she had over at Wayne State. Some writer woman. Shirley wanted me to go with her. I hadn't heard of her myself. But. Girl, I turned *red*, and you know it take a lot for *me* to turn red. And then she read some travel article she was working on. Well, if you ask me, neither of the stuff need to be read in public."

"Well, what do you expect from those New Yorkers?"

"She's not from New York; she's from this little dingy town

in Ohio or Lord knows where. Lord, you should have heard her
brag about it too. Lord, I almost had a fit."
    "One of those out-of-the-way places?"
    "Out of the way and clear around the corner!"
    "I know what you mean."
    "And bragging about it, honey. I almost had a fit right there.
Shirley kept nudging me. She knew who she was, but I didn't know
her from Eve, and after hearing that stuff, don't want to know
neither. I never heard so much bitch this and bitch that and pussy
whatnot, girl. I'm not kidding. Am I talking too loud? I mean, I
don't talk that dirty when I'm sleeping. I wouldn't even tell my
diary that stuff that she addresses to the general public . . . That
ain't no colored child of mine, as they used to say."
    "I know what you mean."
    "Shirley kept nudging me."
    "What do you know about Ernest? Now that's a doll. If there
ever was a man in the world with the *right name!* Shuger! Genuine
sugar!"
    "Genuine *brown* sugar!"
    "Say it again, girl. I hear you. Anyway, how did he meet that
woman? I know he rues that day."
    "I don't know how they met. But his father is some farmer
from Minnesota, sent him off to U of M med school to become
a doctor—he dropped out and started writing about medicine
instead of practicing it, though from what I hear he know enough
to be a doctor if he wanted to be one. You just don't know about
some folks . . ."
    "Well, there's one he does his practice on . . ."
    "Girl, you're too much. Anyway . . ."
    "Wish it was me."
    "Hear you talking. Anyway, what was I saying? You made me
lose my train."
    "About how he met her."
    "I don't know how he met that woman, but he deserves better

. . . Now, I could put some of these other men with her and say she was their *just* deserts, but not him. I remember I used to have this crush on him my own self. I really don't know how they met, because he wasn't really in our circle, you know. I don't even know if he *had* a circle to tell the truth. Just looked up one day and they were together. Love is weird. Anybody doing a study on *weird love* ought to check them out . . . I don't know what's wrong with that woman. Any other woman. Catch like that. I don't know what keeps some people together."

"We all expected so much from her. Change art. Change the world. I always liked her, but she was one of those people with that morally superior air about them all the time. You know. *Too* idealistic."

"We were all too idealistic."

"Yeah, you know, but even in that she was sort of off. None of us could make up our minds about her. Outsider among outsiders, that's what Mejia used to call her. Oh, she was *with* us, but . . . Well, there was a group of us who *loved her*, and another group that thought she behaved like her shit don't stink. But she used to get so mad at all of us, our in-fighting and pettiness—and girl we could be *petty*—she'd say that we behaved like we were fighting windmills when it was giants we were fighting."

"That sounds like her."

"Now that Mejia used to get off a little to herself, too, and sort of sit back and look like she was being amused . . ."

"Yeah, but she was from Colombia, one of those places, you couldn't expect her to *blend*."

"Had as much booty in her as anybody."

"Yeah well, she did run with us, not like Miss Argentina."

"Yeah, I remember Miss Argentina."

"What was that girl's name?"

"She was from Nicaragua, though, I believe."

"Why did everybody call her Argentina?"

"I don't know."

"Now I know she had more booty in her than me."

"Mejia knew she was Black."

"Uhm hmn."

"I wonder what she's doing now?"

"I wouldn't put it past her being a guerrilla somewhere."

"I hope she don't disappear down there. A lot of people's disappearing."

"Somebody said that Loyola went down to Colombia to take pictures."

"No, she's *at* Columbia, teaching photography. I know that to be true."

"Tell me something."

"Well, I know that Mejia's got to be a guerrilla. That's why she was probably so amused at us all the time. Playing revolutionaries when she knew Che."

"No, she didn't know Che, but she actually met his brother Raul though. Can you believe it?"

"Uhm uhm. Suppose it *is* her?"

"I bet she goes to pieces. Look at her."

"Ernie looks good though."

"You can say that again. Wish he'd remember one of us and slide over here."

Glass, stone, nails, wrenches, drills: things I cannot use.

"She wouldn't even go to parties, girl. She'd either be badgering us at some rally, writing up some new Black arts manifesto, or working on her painting—like you could fight giants with aesthetics!—it was painting then: it was later she turned to sculpture. Something she wrote about the three-dimensional figure and its relationship to Black aesthetics. Whatever it was I don't see any of it in what she's doing now!"

"My father used to say some people just don't know how to handle disappointment. I think that's what it is. I just believe she doesn't know how to handle disappointment."

"Disappointment? What's she got to be disappointed about? I wish I had half of what she has. Wish I had the whole of that man though!"

"Don't you know . . . But in herself, I meant. In what she expected out of Catherine."

"I know I expected something else. If that is her, I don't believe it. Is that her?"

The Letter Opener

He opened his eyes and I was holding the letter opener right in front of his neck. He just opened his eyes and looked at the letter opener and looked at me. He turned over on his side away from me and waited. He gave me some moments to do something if I was going to do it. Then he said, "Do you want to take your shower first or shall I?" Just like it was an ordinary morning, just like he was living with Catherine anywoman.

"I'll take mine first," I said and put the letter opener back in the drawer. When I came back the bed was made and he was standing in his drawers.

"I'm through," I said.

Then he went to the bathroom and took his shower. My medicine was sitting on the night table with a glass of water. I took my medicine and then I looked in the night-table drawer and the letter opener was gone.

He's no fool, you know.

Before I Enter I Know There Are Changes

Before I enter I know there are changes. I know what I do not recognize. I do not recognize anything that will cause harm. I recognize nothing with sharp edges.

"What's wrong?" he asks.

"Nothing," I say.

At night while he is sleeping, I could swallow his air.

But he does not keep me overnight.

Busy Work

"The pass is for only a couple of hours, then I'll have to take you back to the hospital," he says. "Why don't you try to get some work done?"

But I do not. I stand at the worktable and chew my hands.

Do you know why sometimes I'm afraid to hug him?

Amanda Is Sitting Across from Me

One of her eyes is bigger than the other. One of her eyes looks like it has a devil in it and the other, an angel. Amanda is sitting across from me. One of her eyes is bigger than the other. In one there is an angel sitting; in the other, a devil. Is this why I have always liked her?

I'd Grab the Wrong Part

And if I were to catch Ernest in a net like one catches a fox, I'd grab the wrong part of the tail, and he'd turn around and bite me back.

Such a Question

"What do you think about when you and your husband make love?" my shrink asks.

Is it appropriate for her to ask such a question?

But this is America. When one submits to its shrinks, one submits the whole way.

His Shadow

His shadow looks like it's inspecting mine.

Eating Beauty

We were sitting in Gillette's studio eating fish sandwiches and drinking coffee.

"I call that painting *Yeats*," she said. "He was very prophetic. Do you know he predicted the anti-Christ of the year 2000?"

"It wasn't only his prediction," I said.

"Uh, I don't know, but, uh, he predicted it; Christ, though, was the anti-Christ of the Egyptians. So to speak."

I removed a small fishbone from my tongue.

"I haven't read much Yeats, except the Crazy Jane poems."

"Do you like Goethe?"

"Yes."

"I call that piece '*I too have had moments of fancifulness.*' I don't know if the critics will get the allusion; they'll just get the sex like they did on that last piece. I'd like to be called intelligent just once. X's erotic and they call him intelligent all the time."

I said nothing. I bit into another piece of fish.

"With us it's either one or the other. But I love using literary allusions in art, like little puzzles, you see, like little codes . . . I hope you won't be mad at me for saying this?"

"Saying what?"

"Well, it's just that you don't have any really *great* literature, so to speak, so you can't really use any *great* literary allusions in your work, if you thought to do it."

I bit into bone.

"Well, I suppose you could use the music. The jazz is great, the spirituals. I never can really get into soul. I don't like it. But the music, I guess that could be good for allusion in your work—Coltrane influencing your sculpture—that's real neat, don't you think? Or some of the great sermons, like Martin Luther King's. I suppose that. But I wonder how you'd do it, don't you? I don't know how you'd quite compete with that."

I pick another fishbone from my tongue. Bone her.

"Maybe I ought to listen to some Coltrane myself!" She laughs.

She's standing at her worktable and I'm sitting in a small antique rocker.

"You're very sweet to be here and keep me company when there's your own work," she says. "Uh, you're so quiet. What is it?"

"I don't know. I just get moody sometimes. There's nothing."

"Uh, I know what you mean. If I'm not moody, I'm into rages. And sometimes, sometimes I don't know where I am."

"You paint better than most artists who know where they are."

"Well, thanks. I like that, coming from you."

"Why do you call that piece *Eating Beauty*? Is that a literary allusion too?"

She laughs. "No. My folks think I'm crazy to try to be an artist. I tell them I want to make beauty. They tell me you can't eat beauty. That's why I call this piece *Eating Beauty*. See?"

I nod. She paints it with a plumber's helper. You know what that is. It looks like one big pussy. The painting, not the plumber's helper. Well, maybe the plumber's helper too.

"They think I'm wicked and selfish because I don't want to marry and have children, like the other girls in our town, but that would just kill my work, you know. When you have a kid, it means you're ready to give up."

"I don't believe that."

"Believe it, Cathy. And I'm not ready to give up, not by a long shot. And I'll never be ready to give up!" She twisted her hair in her fingers, brushed a handful behind her ear. "I'd never kill my work on account of some guy or some kid. No indeed. I'd kill *them* first . . . You think I'm crazy, don't you?"

"No," I mumble.

"But you'll get married, Cathy," she exclaims. "Oh, you *will*, and you'll have lots of kids and you'll . . ."

"I won't give up."

"Oh, yes you will, Cathy. You will. Do you know why you will?"

"Why?"

"Because you're not bitchy enough."

I stare at her.

"Because you should have told me to go to hell back there telling you how you should do your work and you didn't!"

Aren't You Going to
Introduce Me to the Artist?

"Aren't you going to introduce me to the artist?"

"Oh, Catherine, this is one of our noted art historians."

"Marvelous, marvelous. Reminds me of the things the Cree—are they the Cree?—do with their canoes, the carvings, so eloquent, and so primitive. Do I detect some Gillette Viking influence here? You should watch out for that girl; she's a monster." He rubs his hands together. "Ah, now this, this is the kind of art that I like. I really love it. I could eat it." He smacks his lips. "Well, this is certainly a marvelous show. Don't you keep her all to yourself. Let her mingle."

"I'm trying to get her to join some of us for a reception out at the ranch, but she won't come."

"She won't come?"

"No, she won't come."

"Well, it's certainly a marvelous show; it's certainly shed some new light on her work for me. I still think that *Birdcatcher* piece deals with a woman's sexual fate. But what do I know? I'm just an art historian." He winks at me.

I hold my glass of sherry against my waist.

"Don't let art historians fool you," says the director.

"You ought to come out to the ranch," says the historian.

"No, my husband's waiting for me at the hotel."

"You're married? You still look like a little girl. But make him wait." Hand on my arm.

"Go to hell."

He mutters and wanders off.

Introducing Gwendola

She sits in the hall. She looks like she's exploring one hand with the other. When you walk by her, you say hi, but you don't ask questions.

Portrait

Her nose looks powdered, but the rest of her face is shiny.

The Gallery Director Shows Surprise

The gallery director shows surprise.
   "I'm Catherine Shuger," I say.
   "You're Catherine Shuger?"

I dreamed that Gillette and I went to the gallery at the same time.
   The gallery director walked through me to get to Gillette.
   "Ah, you must be Catherine Shuger."
   "No," Gillette pouted. "That's Catherine Shuger."
   The gallery director turned but could not find her way back through me.

That Time Ern Saw Something

That time Ern saw something Gillette had done. In this book on modern art. We thumbed through it.

"She's good, ain't she?"

I don't tell him I know her.

"I think she's very good," he repeated.

They didn't have her picture, just her work.

"I think this one's better." I pointed to another.

"Oh, she's a hellavuh lot better than that."

What do catbirds do?

"Are you in here?"

I find me.

"Why'd you let them put this in there? That's your worst piece. Make you seem light."

Ambition, or Hearing the Bitch

"I don't just have some minor dream," says Gillette.

"What do you mean?"

She punches at her canvas with her brush.

"I want them to call me the best," she sighs. "Well, at least of my generation. I'd like to at least be the best of my generation." She laughs. "Is that ambition enough for you?

When she says ambition, you can hear the bitch.

Dear Amanda Mariner Wordlaw,

Didn't think I knew your maiden name, did you, kid?

You were a real fucker not to come with us. But there you are on your sunny island anyway. I was thinking yesterday about that bullshit you told me about showing off—about my wanting the show—about my doing what I do to show off. But that really applies to you, dear. We were a *show* for you—when we got to be boring, when my attempts weren't imaginative enough, when we got to be a movie you'd seen too much of, and when you thought you really had to do some serious *participating* in our real life—when you thought we'd really *catch* you—you took to your heels, so to speak.

But I can see you now, sitting in that peacock chair, scribbling your shit—or down at the beach looking for some new beauty to pick! And send me my notebook, girl—I know you've had your hands on that!

By the way, I've met your Lantis and your Panda. What a nice little girl! Speaking of someone worth being loved! And your man! I spent a whole evening with the two of them, and they were eager (anxious?) to know that you were safe and sound. You really don't know what beauty is at all, do you? You think it's something you can eat. (If you've had your hands on my book, you know what I mean.) Once you called me a weird bitch—well, you'd better join our ranks, kiddo!

I know Ern was starting to think of you as the better woman, but you're not; you're just another fucked-up brat. Maybe you should have come along and fucked each other silly, if that's what it led to. That's what the people thought you were doing anyhow. Or maybe we could have had one of those barroom brawls, like you see in those Old West movies, speaking of your cowgirls. I can picture us rolling around on somebody's floor, and Ern just sitting there and smiling. Give him some relief, huh? Maybe I should have gone after you. So how do you like your mushrooms?

But for him not to see who you really were! The reason you wouldn't believe what that "razor blade" woman did is because you're afraid of what you could be capable of your own funky self. (I know who mailed me that glass bird!)

Another thing. I went to see one of our Gillette's new exhibitions. I didn't go the day they said she'd show up, didn't want to surprise or scare her. Didn't you write somewhere where they were the same thing: surprise and fear? Anyway, someone must've told her I was there, because she sent me this postcard asking me to come spend some time with her. Can you believe that? She's got to know I know. She's off to Morocco, Amsterdam, Paris and wonders if I'd like to come along. Maybe traveling alone scares her. Can you picture me a part of her entourage? But anyway, as I was looking at her paintings I got to thinking: She just might be the best of our generation. She just might be. But then, considering our generation . . . Nothing to kill for, huh?

From one weird bitch to another

Yours truly,
Catherine Peacock Shuger

Epilogue

I slept with my back to Lantis. At first we slept with our backs to each other. Then he turned toward me and put his hand on my shoulder.

"What kind of woman are you?" he asked softly.

"I don't know what kind," I said.

"Don't give me that bullshit about going to find yourself."

"I won't give you that bullshit," I said. Anyway, I already had myself. Didn't we all already have ourselves, for better or worse?

Pressure on my shoulder made me turn to face him.

"Manda-Panda?" he asked.

"What?"

"Can't we do better than this? Can't we do better than this?"

I said nothing.

"I never imagined this," he said.

If I'd written the scene, my next line might have been him saying he should have kept his trap shut, and her saying that he was too honest a man for that, and—

"I never imagined it either," she said instead.

SCRAP THIS AND START OVER

Prologue

When the young man in the café looked up, he smiled at me. I just saw him briefly from the patio, but he was the most handsome young man I've ever seen. Dark black eyes, brown skin, black hair. Features as if they were chiseled, supernatural.

I went over to his table.

"Are you the young man that saved my friend's life?" I asked.

"I saved your friend's life?"

"That woman you pulled out of the water—I'm her friend."

When the waiter came, I ordered an espresso and sat down at the table with the boy.

I call him a boy because he was no more than twenty-three years old—for me, that's a boy these days. His arms in the short-sleeved white shirt were slim, but he looked very strong.

"Oh, that," he said. "She says I saved her, but when she went down and I swam over to her, I couldn't find her. I dived but still couldn't find her. Suddenly this woman was clutching my calf. She really fought to be saved, and I pulled her up. She saved herself, if you ask me."

I drank my espresso.

"How do you feel in your skin?"

"I don't understand, Senora. What do you mean?"

I am always Senora, always.

The young man is still looking at me with dark, calm eyes.

"What do you mean, Senora?"

"How does it feel," I ask, "to be the most beautiful man in the world?"